Horace Elisha Scudder

Henry Oscar Houghton

a biographical outline

Horace Elisha Scudder

Henry Oscar Houghton
a biographical outline

ISBN/EAN: 9783743306226

Manufactured in Europe, USA, Canada, Australia, Japa

Cover: Foto ©Raphael Reischuk / pixelio.de

Manufactured and distributed by brebook publishing software
(www.brebook.com)

Horace Elisha Scudder

Henry Oscar Houghton

HENRY OSCAR HOUGHTON

A Biographical Outline

BY

HORACE E. SCUDDER

CAMBRIDGE
Printed at the Riverside Press
M DCCC XCVII

PREFACE

WHEN the family of Mr. Houghton asked me to prepare a memorial of his life I gladly consented, for it was a grateful task to recall his vigorous personality. I did not fully perceive till I came to write my book how impossible it would be to make anything like an adequate Life: there were very few letters which I could use, for almost the whole of Mr. Houghton's correspondence was of a business sort, and it was difficult to detach him from his business. I was bent on presenting him individually, yet some of his most notable achievements were accomplished through and with the hearty coöperation of his associates. I am sure they will not misunderstand the concentration of my attention on him.

I was compelled, after I had sketched the

beginning of his life by means of such scanty
documents as I could procure, to rely largely
upon my own recollections and impressions.
The portrait thus is drawn from my own
point of view. It is no more than an outline. If conditions had been more favorable,
not only would I gladly have filled out the
sketch with a more detailed treatment, but I
would have tried to correct my own view by
a comparison with that of one and another of
Mr. Houghton's acquaintances and friends.
In truth I fear I have strayed somewhat from
the task set me of preparing a memorial volume. I can only plead that after thirty years'
constant intercourse with Mr. Houghton, his
personality was too vivid for me to treat it
with the studied impartiality of a historian.

NOTE ON THE PORTRAITS

THE frontispiece is from a photograph taken in 1893 for use by Mr. Robert Gordon Hardie when painting the portrait presented by Mr. Houghton to his partners and associates, which hangs in the Counting Room of the Riverside Press.

The picture facing page 12 represents Mr. Houghton just before entering college, and his sister Marilla, afterwards Mrs. Gallup, who was two years his junior.

The portrait facing page 56 gives the aspect of Mr. Houghton at the time when he went into business with Mr. Bolles.

The three-quarters portrait opposite page 74 is from a photograph taken about 1860.

The figure which faces page 82 is from a photograph taken in Paris when Mr. Houghton was there in 1864.

The portrait opposite page 110 is from a photograph taken in 1878.

In the Aldermanic Chamber at the City Hall, Cambridge, hangs a painting by Mr. Hardie which was presented to the city by various persons engaged in the business of the Press, and at the several offices of Houghton, Mifflin and Company. The photogravure facing page 132 is from this painting, and Mr. Hardie in executing the portrait had before him a photograph taken by Sarony about 1884.

The latest portrait of Mr. Houghton is that facing page 152, and is from a photograph taken in 1895.

HENRY OSCAR HOUGHTON

I

HENRY OSCAR HOUGHTON was born on the 30th of April, 1823, in Sutton, a hill town of Caledonia County, in the northeastern corner of Vermont. His mother, who was forty-three years old at the time, was Marilla, daughter of Captain James Clay, of Putney, Vermont, an officer in the Revolutionary army. His father, six years his wife's senior, was Captain William Houghton, a native of Bolton, Massachusetts. Bolton had been set off from Lancaster, and Lancaster had been the home of the Houghton family since John Houghton, of Lancaster, England, came to America in the Abigail in 1635. Captain William Houghton was somewhat of a rover, and took his growing family with him as he moved from one place to another up the Connecticut valley and into the Vermont hills, and even,

when his children had begun to establish
themselves, into the southwest part of New
York State.

There were six sons and six daughters, and
a period of nearly twenty-one years separated
Henry Oscar, who was the youngest but one,
from his sister Stella, who was the oldest in
the family. Of the six sons, two became
clergymen, one died in his early manhood,
two were merchants, and the youngest was
the printer and publisher. He had one sister
younger than himself, Marilla Houghton, who
became a teacher, married Dr. J. C. Gallup,
and established the large girls' school in
Clinton, New York, now known as Houghton
Seminary. Mr. Houghton outlived all his
brothers and sisters, but during their lifetime
his relations with them were very close. He
was, at one time, under the watch and ward
of his brother Daniel, eight years his senior;
his brother Albert Gallatin became his business partner in 1866; he owed much to his
oldest sister and her husband, David Scott,
and the long period when he and his younger
sister were the only ones left made the connec-

tion between them one of special tenderness. The family scattered widely, five of the members going to Alabama; but when the youngest son was born no one was yet married, and probably all were gathered in the home at Sutton.

Sutton is high up on one of the long lines of rolling hills which run north and south. It looks off upon Burke Mountain in the southeast and the Willoughby Gap about six miles to the northeast. The Gap and Lake form strikingly picturesque points in the landscape, but otherwise the country is not marked by more noticeable features than the hills which one climbs only to find other hills lying beyond. The country is a farming and grazing district, and has changed little since the Houghton family lived there. The plain house in which Mr. Houghton was born still stands in the village, and there are persons living who remember the little shock-headed boy, with hair hanging over his forehead, who made one of the figures in the household.

Captain Houghton moved to Sutton in 1820. It was one of the resting-places in his roving life. He was a tanner by trade, but had failed in business in Lyndon, his previous home, and seems to have gained his livelihood in Sutton by working for the farmers there. The family was large and it was a hard struggle to keep the wolf from the door. That the worst did not befall them was due largely to the energy and thrift of the mother, whom her son often spoke of with admiration for her force of character. The Houghtons did not strike root very deeply in the thin soil of Sutton, and, after a few years, once more moved on to Bradford. In one of his addresses before the Vermont Association, Mr. Houghton gave a slight reminiscence of this time of his early youth.

"When I was a very small boy, not over ten years old," he said, "my family emigrated from the northern part of Vermont, from the little town of Sutton, a famous maple-sugar town, to the town of Bradford, on the Connecticut River; and my duty on that journey, besides riding on the furniture wagon, was to help drive the cows which we had to take with us. One Saturday evening, just at dusk, we came to the little town of Ryegate, and the signs of thrift and industry, as shown by the green fields, attracted my father, so that he stopped at what was then a Scotch village. I remember that I was frightened nearly out of my wits by the landlady, who, while stirring her oatmeal porridge, complained volubly because we did not go on to the next tavern. So fearful and depressed was I that I could not taste of that wonderful dish, which, they say, is 'the food of horses in England, and of men in Scotland.' But when I was lighted up to bed by the landlord's daughter, as she handed me the candle to go to my little chamber, she put her soft hand on my head, — and I have felt the sympathetic touch of that soft hand for over fifty years." The reminiscence was used in introducing a reference to Mr. Whitelaw Reid, whose mother was a native of Ryegate, but it was indicative of a nature singularly susceptible to little kindnesses.

At Bradford there was a country academy, and here the boy had for three years his schooling, but at thirteen began to earn his living by binding himself as apprentice in the office of the *Free Press*, at Burlington, then owned by H. B. Stacy, where he served for six years. Mr. Houghton liked in a quiet way to observe anniversaries; and when he was in Vermont in 1894, he visited the *Free Press* office in Burlington on the 27th of October, and stood by the window where, on that same day fifty-eight years before, he took his place at the case as an apprentice. Of his first journey from his home into the world, where he was to make his way at first on foot, as it were, he wrote, nearly sixty years after : —

" On October 26, 1836, hours before dawn, I started in the mail-coach from Bradford, on the Connecticut River, for Burlington, on Lake Champlain, to be initiated into a knowledge of printing, an occupation which I have followed chiefly since that time until the present, and am still in my humble way engaged in it. On the way over the hills from Bradford to Montpelier, a heavy snow-storm was falling, and the apple-trees were loaded with frozen apples. At high noon of that day we halted for dinner in this village [Montpelier], then as now the capital of the State. I remember with what wonder my boyish eyes looked upon the State House, then standing on this site, with its tall columns, and with what admiration they rested on the member from my native town, dressed in the traditional blue coat with brass buttons, the usual apparel of statesmen of that day, so very different from the farmer's frock in which I had been accustomed to see him in his native village. Many hours after dark we arrived in Burlington, having made a journey of eighty miles during the day."

It was while he was in the printing-office that he had an encounter which he liked to relate in after years for its curious connection with a large interest in his business life. One day a pale, slim man came into the office, and showed the young compositor a printed list of words which he carried with him. "My lad," he said, "when you use these words, will you please spell them according to this list?" — *theater*, *center*, and the like. It was Noah Webster, who was traveling about the coun-

try, and, with the shrewdness which sent him
to the censors of spelling, was visiting the
printing-offices, and persuading the compositors to adopt his reforms. Webster had
already published his dictionary, but the
young printer was to be one of the principal
agents in making the book in its ultimate
form the great handbook of the American
people.

Captain Houghton and his family had mean-
while made another move to Nunda Valley,
in Livingston County, New York; but Daniel
Houghton was a student in the University of
Vermont, at Burlington, where he was looking
forward to the life of a clergyman. He kept
a brotherly watch over the young apprentice,
and stood to him very much *in loco parentis.*
There is a letter by him to his mother, written
in June, 1839, which carries with it a very
distinct air of authority. His father was at
the time in Bradford, and the mother and son
seemed to be arranging in his absence what
should be done about the boy's education.

"Maria mentioned," Daniel Houghton
writes, "that you would like to have Oscar

come home and go to school there a year. Did I know that you had a good school, a preceptor amply competent to teach the classics, I should have no objections to his going. I wish to have him fit for college; he might possibly do it in one year, but it probably will be better for him not to enter until two years from August. I intend to have him go to school steady after next August, whether he goes home or not. The only objection to his going home would be that the advantages would not be as good as here, and the expense of the journey. Should it be desirable to have him at home a year, and should the school be suitable, I have no objections to have him go home in the fall. Please inform me respecting the school, — whether the teacher is a graduate and of what college, etc."

The work in the printing-office confirmed the young apprentice in rudimentary knowledge, and after a long day spent in manual labor he applied himself to books in the evening, but in the fall of 1839 it was decided that he should go home to Nunda and enter the academy there. He appears to have spent at least two years there and at Wyoming, for another migration of the family had shifted the scene from Nunda to Portage, near Wyoming. How much he was master of himself at this time is curiously evident in a bundle of faded boyish compositions, translations, and exercises in a debating club. Both the handwriting and the spelling bear testimony to the influence upon him of his work at type-setting, and, though the literary form is not altogether smooth, there is a vigor and independence in the thought which indicates a good degree of maturity and self-reliance. It strikes one as felicitous that he should be writing with determination on Decision of Character, — an essay which interested him so much that he produced a " revised edition " a couple of months later ; and that he should have amused himself, in a composition on the New Year, with the following calculation : —

"Perhaps we might very profitably, as we commence the new year, look back and see how we have spent the old one. Allowing seven hours for sleep, there are seventeen hours in each day to be improved in some way or other; and, allowing another three hours for work or play (as the case may be), we have fourteen hours left, about half of which we generally spend in school; and probably there are not many of us, if any, who study more than four hours out of school, which leaves three hours in each day unaccounted for, and, not reckoning Sundays, we have 313 days in a year; and, losing at the rate of three hours in each day, at the end of the year we should come out *minus* thirty-nine days and three hours, and in *ten* years something over a whole year; and, taking into consideration the maxim that 'time is money,' we might suppose each hour to be worth a sixpence, which would amount in one year to $58.68¼, and in ten years to $586.87½."

II

APPARENTLY, the year before entering college was spent again at the case in Burlington, but in the fall of 1842, when he was nineteen years old, he was able to pass an examination and enter the University of Vermont. He used to say that he had three York shillings in his pocket when he entered college, two of which he used for getting himself in order in his room, leaving twelve and a half cents for further expenses. But he had been inured to hardship, he had perforce acquired the most frugal habits, and he had the very great advantage of familiarity with a craft which gave him considerable support as he worked his way through college. He was, however, chiefly indebted for his support to the generous aid of Mr. David Scott, who had married his sister Stella, and was engaged in business in Alabama. He used in later life to illustrate the stringency of his means at

this time by telling how he received a letter on which the postage had not been prepaid. Between his absolute lack of the needed twenty-five cents and his resentment at being forced by his correspondent to pay, he was inclined to refuse the letter; but curiosity and hope conspired to defeat his pride, and he borrowed the money, opened the letter, and found it contained money from his brother-in-law, or at any rate a promise of aid. The following extracts from letters written by Mr. Scott to his young brother-in-law during these years will indicate, brief as they are, not only the ready aid which he gave, but the generous spirit and the friendly counsel accompanying the aid: —

September 1, 1843. — " A letter from Stella after she arrived at Dana, Massachusetts, tells me that you are straitened for funds to progress in your college course. If you will inform me what amount is necessary to carry you through, I will endeavor to assist you. In a few months exchanges will be down, and I can then remit you the necessary sums from time to time to defray your expenses, which you can refund at your convenience. . . .

"I am in hopes you will improve your time, and when you get through college come South and get into business of some kind."

April, 1844. — "I enclose twenty dollars in South Carolina money, which is the best I can find at present. I hope it will relieve your present difficulties as long as it will last. I shall be pleased to hear from you frequently, how you are getting along, and it will afford me pleasure to assist you from time to time as you may stand in need. Do not be backward in letting your wants be known."

1845. — "I enclose $50; let me know when you will stand in need of more funds.

"Please acknowledge the receipt of this amount.

"It will be necessary for you to study bookkeeping, so as to understand accounts. If you could improve the appearance of your handwriting, it would be desirable."

The University of Vermont at that time was a modest institution, with the Rev. Dr.

John Wheeler for President, and a Faculty
of half a dozen professors, of whom the Rev.
Joseph Torrey, Professor of Intellectual and
Moral Philosophy, was perhaps the most eminent. There was a library of about ten thou-
sand volumes, and the body of students did
not much exceed a hundred in number. But
no one who knows the spirit of our New England colleges in the early half of this century
will be disposed to measure the worth of the
training received by the meagreness of equip-
ment or the paucity of numbers. The University of Vermont, like other New England
colleges, took its impress from a few controlling spirits, and, at the time when Mr.
Houghton was in Burlington, the Marsh
family was a prominent factor in collegiate
life, and James Marsh was the prophet of
Coleridge in America. It is a coincidence
that one of Mr. Houghton's contemporaries
at college, a young instructor then, afterward
the well-known Professor W. G. T. Shedd,
became, through the same influence, the
American editor of Coleridge's writings, and
that one of the latest enterprises in which

Mr. Houghton took an active interest was the
publication in America of Coleridge's *Letters.*
He was unmistakably affected in his judgment by the strong attraction this writer had
for him in college days. There was a philosophical and theological bent given to the
minds of students at that time, which is apparent in the system of education followed in
the University. As if to justify such a name
for the institution, the studies were divided
into four departments, under the names of
the Department of English Literature, the
Department of Languages, the Department of
Mathematics and Physics, and the Department
of Political, Moral, and Intellectual Philosophy, which comprised recitations and lectures
in Political Economy, the Principles and Forms
of Government, Laws of Nature and Nations,
Ethics, Natural Theology, and Evidences of
Revealed Religion, Logic, and Metaphysics.
In later life Mr. Houghton was a strong advocate of the country college. He was pre-
judiced in its favor no doubt by the fact of
his own history, but a strong ground for his
confidence lay in his recognition of the per-

sonal force exerted by a few men of power upon a small body of students, and especially of the gradual convergence of prescribed courses toward an ultimate philosophical statement of the doctrines which should furnish the young student with a rational law of living.

The records of the University library give some indication of the character of the reading in which Mr. Houghton engaged independently of his regular college work. It is a meagre list for the four years, not more than thirty books in all; and some of these were clearly direct aids to prescribed study. It is probable that, with his irregular preparation for college and his necessity to eke out his means with labor, he had little leisure for many excursions in literature; but the quality of his reading shows the man who throve on a strong diet. The first book he took out in his Freshman year was the first volume of Winthrop's *History of New England*, following it shortly with a two-volume work by Charles Mills on the *History of the Crusades*. A long gap, from the middle of

October to the middle of March, was closed
by William Godwin's *Enquirer*, and before
the year closed he had taken out three volumes of Dr. Johnson's writings, Tanner's
*Narrative of Adventures among the Indi-
ans*, and two volumes of Leighton's works.
In his Sophomore year he appears to have
drawn but a single book, a volume of Shake-
speare; in his Junior year his reading was
mainly in ancient and English history. His
Senior year shows half the entire list: he was
making his way in Scotch metaphysics, but he
was also reading Kent's *Commentaries*, Milton's prose works, Butler's *Analogy*, Fénelon,
and Bacon's works. When recalling his college days, he was wont to speak of Milton in
his prose writings as having a strong influence on his intellectual life, especially with regard to the theological problems which he was
engaged in solving; he pondered at times the
expediency of issuing a library edition of Milton's prose; he looked forward to publishing
Leighton in his *Library of Old Divines*, and
there were few of his publications in which he
took greater pride than the edition of Bacon's

works edited by James Spedding, reprinted by him at the outset of his publishing career, upon terms which made Mr. Spedding a warm advocate of American publishers' modes of business.

With the package of school compositions is another of similar essays written during the college course. Some of them help to explain the choice of books from the college library, and the subjects have somewhat the air of having been assigned by a college officer. "The Idea of Liberty among the Ancient Greeks," "The Study of the Classics," "Importance of Mathematical Studies," "Beauty of Thought makes Beauty of Style," "What is Education," are the set pieces in the old-fashioned display of collegiate pyrotechnics. But now and then there is a phrase, a turn of thought, a whole paper it may be, which has a personal interest as showing how the young student thought and felt, or what was engaging his mind. The presidential election which occurred in his Junior year was that in which Clay played the losing game against Polk. The tariff of 1842 had become a party watchword, and the annexation of Texas was a burning question. Like many other ardent young men of his day, Mr. Houghton was an enthusiastic follower of Clay, and he was old enough to have shared in the slogan of "Tippecanoe and Tyler too," and to have shared likewise in the disappointment over Tyler's defection. In one of his college essays he defines his political position. "One of the parties," he says, "as it seems to me, has fixed its stand upon principles, while the other has broken away, in a measure, from all principle, and seeks to build it all up by flattering the caprices of the multitude. The one advocates a sound national currency, protection to home industry, and an equitable distribution of the sales of the public lands; while the other sets forth no principles definitely, but promises to do everything well, if the people will only let them have the power. During the administration of the government for five or six years previous to 1840 [when the Whigs came into power under Harrison], the country was compelled to undergo a series of changes, experiments, and expedients, when the whole nation arose in its might and shook off its thralldom. But, seeing its anticipations all blasted, it sank back into lethargy. But now, hope having dawned upon it once more, the whole country is rising at the 'blast of the bugle' which is being reëchoed from Maine to Georgia, and from Boston harbor to the Mississippi."

He devoted one of his compositions to an inquiry into the policy of annexing Texas. His argument against annexation was based on the moral weakness which overtook nations when they turned their attention to the extension of territory, rather than to the development of internal resources. Such lust of power, he maintains, leads to party strife and distraction within the state itself; and, after citing Greece, Rome, and England, he suddenly turns for an instance of comparison to Delaware and New York, "the former of which is one of the smallest States in the Union, is out of debt, and seems to be thriving, from the fact that she is not torn by sectional interests. The latter is one of the largest, and possesses, perhaps, a greater variety of resources than any other State in the Union. But at one time she is embarking largely in internal improvements ; at another she is stopping her public works, and allowing them to go to ruin when well-nigh completed. Now she is borrowing money to defray the expenses of government, now levying a direct tax to pay her debts, just as sectional interests or parties predominate.

" The interests of every part of the Union at the present time seem to be at war with each other, but it is so equally balanced that it is confidently hoped that there will always be a sufficient number of the wise and honorable in our national councils to prevent one portion of the Union triumphing over another. But add the foreign territory of Texas to our Union, and the worst results are to be feared from the clashing of sectional interests, — nothing less than anarchy and disunion, and when that day arrives it will be truly said that ' our glory has departed.' "

The turn of the argument is a characteristic one, for Mr. Houghton often showed in discussion a curious faculty for seizing upon some illustration whose pertinency was not

immediately apparent, but which, by some
involution of his mind, had an effectiveness
for him, and served by its picturesqueness or
other striking quality to drive home the point
he was making. His Commencement part was
upon " The Necessity and True Method of a
System of State Education." It is interesting
to notice, that though he drew from the college library Grimke on *Education* and an *Ab-
stract of Massachusetts School Reports* for
the years 1838–1840, his oration began with a
quotation from Bacon, took in Milton by the
way, and showed the influence of Coleridge in
the closing paragraph.

" Since the state is admitted to have a moral
being, with moral attributes and a moral character, the system of education which it adopts
should be nothing else but a means of self-
education; and this must be limited and directed, as has been intimated, by the wants
which it feels. If, then, it would have a continued and healthful growth, it will strive to
know its own wants, and will use, as far as
possible, the means to satisfy them. Its physical wants every nation feels to a greater or

less extent; but the higher wants which belong to the intellectual and moral nature are not so soon awakened, and for that very reason, when they begin to be felt, their claims assume a paramount importance. The highest energies of the state should be directed to their satisfaction; since, by seeking the highest moral and intellectual culture of all its members, it will inevitably seek its own, so that in the state and the individual will be realized the vision of the prophet, ' whose appearance and work was, as it were, a wheel in the middle of a wheel, and whithersoever the spirit went the wheels went, for the spirit of the living creature was in the wheels.' "

The class of 1846, of which Mr. Houghton was a member, contained in its last year twenty-four students, and of that number about a fourth are still living, fifty years after graduation. One of the number, Mr. Neziah Wright Bliss, at the time hailing from Bradford, and now a resident of Chicago, has kindly given me his recollections of his fellow-student. He had known the Houghton family in Bradford; indeed, a sister of his at one time was engaged to be married to a brother of Mr. Houghton. Oscar Houghton he had known but slightly, since he was but a boy when he left Bradford.

"Some days," Mr. Bliss says, "or perhaps weeks, after my entering with the Freshman class of 1842 at Burlington, a tall young man, slim and very much bent or bowed, as homely of feature as Abraham Lincoln, and as awkward and ungainly in person and manners, came up to me on the campus, and asked if I was Nezi Bliss (my name is Neziah) of Bradford, telling me he was Oscar Houghton. Of course I knew all about him at once (as to his antecedents), and was glad to know him again. I was very small for my age (I was then sixteen), and, having been prepared to enter a year before (but remained at the academy a year longer on account of size as much as age), I was unusually well prepared for those days. Several of my former classmates at the academy were then Sophomores at various colleges, — one now Rev. O. T. Lanphear, at Burlington. I found that Oscar had been, in fact was then, a type-setter in a printing-office, and was so poorly prepared to enter college that he could barely squeeze in. The reason for this was entirely legitimate : he had to support himself, while preparing to enter college, by an industry that was not very lucrative ; and he had to attend the academy as he could, and oftentimes study by himself without instructors. All this he told me, and, without in any way announcing any boastful determination, said he was going to try it and see if he could catch up and keep up ; that it would be hard work, as he would still have his living to make, as well as his tuition and expenses of text-books and clothing to meet. In entering, he registered himself as of Portage, New York, which was doubtless the place to which his father's family removed from Bradford, and his room the first year was No. 4 South College ; the next year he roomed and boarded at Mrs. Coon's ; the third year he again roomed in college (North College, No. 2), registering those two years as of Burlington ; but in our Senior year he roomed at Mr. Cook's, and registered as of Dana, Massachusetts, and so wrote his name and place of birth, as well as date, in my autographs of the class. Of course, under these adverse circumstances, Mr. Houghton's beginnings in the class were inconspicuous, and little attention was paid to him at first by the class generally, in which were a considerable number of well-prepared students of mature age, notably Aiken and Lull, Belcher and Divoll, Hitchcock and Jameson, May and Prentiss, Stebbings and Wainwright, and later Nelson; but being a personal friend, I could not but notice, and did notice, how gradually, day by day and week by week, Oscar Houghton was gaining and growing, delivering better recitations and becoming better known to his class, more, I am convinced, by his inveterate goodnature and his sterling honesty and integrity than by his increase in scholarship. It was the custom for all the students of that day to attend prayers in the chapel at sunrise and sunset the year round, and religious services at the chapel at first, and later at the White Church (so called), unless a permit had been obtained to attend elsewhere. I obtained a permit to attend St. Paul's Episcopal Church, then in charge of Bishop Hopkins, a man of great force. Houghton, being a member of the Methodist Church at Burlington, of course attended there. One Sunday he invited me to go with him to church, which I did, and found carpeted aisles, cushioned seats, chandeliers, an upholstered pulpit, and a fashionably dressed, beribboned and bejeweled audience. I was taken by surprise, as the Methodists of my native town insisted on the rule of excessive plainness and simplicity, and on making the seats, as well as psalms, penitential. I called Oscar's attention to the difference, and asked if he was sure of the place. He was embarrassed, but got out of the dilemma by explaining that, even in the Methodist Church, what was the enforced rule in poorer neighborhoods could not be enforced in wealthier ones.

"At that time there were only two public societies in the college, the Phi Sigma Nu and the University Institute, and the practice was, after sufficient time had elapsed, for the upper classes to form some estimate of the character and capacities of the Freshmen, to take the class list, and for the society, which for that year had the choice, to select the first or second name on the list, and then take every other one in the list to its end, so that one half of each class went to each society somewhat by lot. Houghton and I both fell to the Phi Sigma Nu. At that time the parties in the societies were divided on the lines of Church or Non-Church, Liberals or Conservatives, but, with the usual exaggeration of college life, were denominated Blues and Bloats. Without any essential reason on either of our parts, Houghton fell to the Blues and I to the Bloats, and my party was in power in holding the offices during our entire college course; but we always elected Houghton to an office, generally that of treasurer, on account of the universal love and respect with which he was regarded, for he never in his life (I believe) made himself offensive in any way to any one. Early in the history of our society life, Oscar Houghton began to take part in the debates. To do so was by no means general; a few members generally were the speakers, and the great mass of members were listeners only. It was as hard, up-hill work for Mr. Houghton to take part in the debates as it

was to work up in his recitations. He was
troubled immensely with what I suppose the
French call *mauvaise honte*. He would get
up, bent over almost in a semicircle, and begin a stammering, hesitating, awkward, lum-
bering speech, but nevertheless always with
a thought or idea at the bottom which he
could not express or get out; he would be
openly laughed at by some and pitied by his
more intimate friends, and he would give up
and sit down, laughing himself with the others
at his own failure, and by that means relieving
both those who laughed and those who pitied
of all embarrassment; but he would soon be
up again, and sooner or later he would some-
how and after a fashion express a thought on
the subject under discussion that would command the attention and respect of all. This
went on in the society and in the class-room,
and not so slowly as you might suppose, because, when we held our Sophomore exhibition, May 16, 1844, Houghton had so
advanced that he was assigned the honorable
place of the closing speech of the afternoon,
his subject being a characteristic one, for the

handling of which he was evidently peculiarly well qualified, to wit, ' The True Ideal of a Manly Character;' while to your late Judge John W. May, the oldest and most accomplished scholar of the class, was assigned the closing address of the evening, his subject being 'Heroism.' At our Junior exhibition, Mr. Houghton opened the evening exercises by an address on ' The Idea of Liberty among the Ancient Greeks,' and again, in our graduation exercises, opened the second session, his subject being ' The Necessity and True Method of a System of State Education.'

" His success and standing in his class in scholarship was equal to, if not greater than, his success as an essayist; and at the close of our college years no man commanded more the respect of the class than did Mr. Houghton, and I am sure no man was so universally esteemed and loved. If I were to estimate the elements of his character which brought to him the great measure of success that was accorded to him in his life, I should say it was his entire and incorruptible honesty and integrity, bred in the bone and reaching clear through, patent upon the face of all his acts. This, supplemented by his exceeding kindness of heart and never-failing good-nature, gave him those advantages that commanded the success he met and deserved. . . .

"And now, Mr. Scudder, I have written to you my impressions of my friend and class-mate, just as I should wish you to have written me had I inquired instead of you, giving you the facts as they were at the time, not undertaking (after the event) to make out any great things as earnests or prognostications of the success afterwards attained. Mr. Houghton never seemed to me, as in the case of some I have known, to set up any special ideal to which he would strive to attain. I don't think he ever thought of 'aiming high,' or particularly of 'aiming' at all, but I do think he quietly and unostentatiously was determined to do as thoroughly and well as he could whatever his hand found to do, and that he in everything and everywhere conscientiously did his work, leaving the consequences to follow as a matter of course, without in any case particularly contemplating them; and I believe it was this that largely commanded the confidence of his business associates in Cambridge, which to an unusual degree contributed to his success. He has gone, but he has left a most fragrant memory among his friends, and to his family a name and a character that will command the utmost respect of all."

To this vivid reminiscence by Mr. Bliss may be added the memorabilia of other of Mr. Houghton's surviving classmates. Mr. William H. Dodge, now of Westboro', Massachusetts, writes: —

"I was not intimately acquainted with Mr. Houghton outside of his immediate college duties, but in the class and lecture room I sat near him during our entire college course. He was one of the older members of our class, being, I think, nearly twenty-four at graduation, and had then a well-developed, steady, reliable, and manly character.

"As I remember him, while not particularly excelling in any department of college study, he never failed or did poor work, but was a well-balanced, all-round, good average student.

His written productions were always heavily
loaded with good, sound sense. Had he spent
less time in the printing-office, working for
money to help pay his expenses, he would
doubtless have taken higher rank in college
work. I think he gave very little if any time
to college games or social pleasures that would
not yield some profit to present or coming
real life-work."

Mr. Horace R. Stebbings, of Chicago, adds
his recollection in these words : —

"I am glad to contribute any information,
however little, in relation to the college life of
my friend Houghton, for he was my friend
and I always called him 'Oscar.' We were
classmates for four years. Our time — his
time especially — was fully occupied. We
had fewer leisure hours together perhaps
than students now have. We often worked
together, however, and saw new things and
realized new relations as a result of our work.
How can I cut it short? Houghton was one
of the most genial, kind-hearted young men of
them all, and hence perhaps I was drawn to
him. It always seemed to me that I was his

welcome companion, — *persona grata* in modern phrase, — and I loved him for that. He was lightly built in frame, and so seemed taller in stature than most; deliberate of speech; of lively intelligence; an earnest, honest, unsophisticated Yankee boy. He was a printer, as you know, and earned money by his art while in college. Most young men of that time ' paddled their own canoe.' He set types, read proof, etc., in fact did almost everything at times, in the printing-office of Chauncy Goodrich, of Burlington, Vermont. There he met Father O'Calligan, an amiable old priest of the town, who wrote books of various sorts, one *Of Usury*. He and Houghton together corrected the proofs. The old gentleman would sometimes get inspired re-reading his own text, and stop the really useful work and consume the time lecturing Houghton, his audience of one, on the topics of the chapters. Houghton said he did n't think it made any difference to him, since he was paid by the hour. The two became really attached to each other, — the one a highly educated, confirmed old Papist, the other a young Protestant student, and a zealous Methodist at that. It always seemed to me a funny relationship, but serves to show how very easy it is to throw away dogma when warm hearts and loving natures meet.

"I remember how we often picked out the Greek together by the roots, and wondéred how far we should ever go to reap the ripe crops that grow out of these. Houghton, like many other students, did not like to be hindered and limited by the study of what seemed to him unimportant details. We were, for instance, put upon an indigestible diet of Greek prosody for a while. Houghton said: 'I wonder if Professor —— thinks I care anything about the feet of those old Greek poets. I care a great deal more about their heads.'"

When Mr. Houghton was seventy years old, a notice of the fact in the press brought a brief note of congratulation to him from another classmate, J. W. Taylor, of Syracuse, New York, in which the writer says: "It must be now near fifty years since I became acquainted with you, daily toiling up the steep ascent of College Hill, in Burlington, to the recitations in Alma Mater. I remember it seemed to me a wonderful achievement that you should be able to set type all day at the case, and still find time to study and make the three trips from down town and back again and have any vitality left! Through the lapse of time I can see the wonderful nerve it required, and the iron will to back it. But the same determined spirit has borne its fruit through these fifty years."

It is pleasant to show the response to this friendly spirit of his classmates, in a letter which Mr. Houghton wrote to Mr. Stebbings, December 1, 1887 : —

4 PARK STREET, BOSTON,
December 1, 1887.

MY OLD FRIEND AND CLASSMATE STEB-BINGS, — I have often thought of you, and was very glad to receive your photograph. I supposed it represented you, although it was very different from the stubbed young man that I knew in college; and I should have responded, but I did not know where to address you, until I met Jameson, who kindly gave me your address, and agreed to be the medium through which I could convey my shadow to you in return for yours. I think it is very pleasant to have the faces of our old friends, even if the gray hairs have begun to show. I think I am a little younger than I was forty years ago when we were together, and I am quite anxious to know whether you retain that umbrella that you broke over the head of the Sophomore who was trying to intrude himself into your room without permission.

I heard that Mr. Bliss was at Burlington this year at Commencement. I think I should have gone there to meet him alone if I had known he was to have been there. I was there a week or more after the Commencement, and heard of him. He and I were great friends in college, and I have always taken a kindly interest in him. I wish he would send me his photograph, and I shall be very glad to retaliate if he should do so. I am glad to believe that both you and he are prospered so far as this world's goods go, and I am delighted with the description of your family. I should be glad to see any of them if they come to Boston, and I should like to take you to my house and show you mine. I have three of the best girls that there are in the country, except yours, and they are a great comfort to me. I have a son also, who is with me in the business, and who has been married a year or more. My son lives in the house he was born in, and my girls are still with me.

Reciprocating heartily your blessings, and hoping we may meet either here or in Chicago, I am, as ever,

Your friend,

H. O. HOUGHTON.

III

WHEN he was graduated from the University of Vermont in 1846, Mr. Houghton was in debt for his education to the amount of $300, but he was equipped for seeking his fortune with a college training, knowledge of a craft, good health, and indomitable energy. His intention, like that of many young graduates, was to take up school-teaching until the way opened for a permanent vocation; and he appears to have had a partial engagement for the winter of 1846–47 to teach in Hardwick, Massachusetts, not far from Dana, where his parents were now residing. But, missing the first opportunity which presented itself, he fell back upon his craft as a printer, and found also a chance to do reporter's work on the Boston *Traveller*. It is not improbable that the steps which led him into printing as a vocation were taken somewhat reluctantly; for a college education was re-

garded in his youth as more distinctly the
entrance upon one of the learned professions
than it is to-day, and the exèrtions and sacri-
fices required for securing such an education
would seem scarcely justified by a mechanical occupation afterward. I never heard Mr.
Houghton speak in this strain, but I have
often heard him set a high value on the disci-
plinary collegiate training of his day, which
supposed hard intellectual labor for four years.
Certainly in his case the effect of this training
upon his success as a printer and captain of
industry was very great. He was not especially dexterous as a mechanic. His work at
the case, to be sure, had given him facility in
setting type, and I recall an odd illustration
of special expertness which his practice had
given him. He had no liking for games, but
when his children were playing the familiar
letter-game, which consists in constructing a
word out of a jumble of letters, he would
take the unassorted letters and arrange them
at once in their proper order. He knew the
parts of a printing-press, but he had not
the skill which some master printers had, as

the late Mr. Welch, for example, to take a
press apart and put it together again. What
he did have, the gift especially of his college
training, was the power, so much more substantial than mere empiricism, to make his
experiments in his head, — to see what he
wished to accomplish, and what means, mechanical or other, were needed to produce the
desired result. This power was unquestion-
ably confirmed by many years of experience,
so that his knowledge of what went to the
making of a good book — paper, ink, cut of
type, presswork — was unhesitating, but it
was a power which sprang rather from the
logical faculty behind the eye than from the
eye and touch ; and it was, as I have said, a
native gift trained and ordered by intellectual discipline.

Another element of success in his vocation
which he brought with him from college was
also a native gift, enhanced in value by collegiate training, — the gift of good taste, that
quality of selection and reserve which lies at
the bottom of genuine success in any mechanic
art that appeals in the last analysis to the cul-

tivated eye and mind. It was an unfailing source of pleasure to him to examine the work of the great Italian printers, whose masters were in turn the artists of the illuminated missals of the days before printing, and he never wearied of inculcating those fundamental principles of good proportion and simplicity which may be traced in all the acceptable work from Aldus down. There was a certain rule of proportion for the printed page, which an architect once formulated for him; it was a rule which mechanically confirmed what his own good taste had fixed independently; and, in any discussion as to a proposed page, he was pretty sure to apply the rule as an authority, but he did not need the rule to satisfy himself: his eye was quite as trustworthy. It was the custom in the office, never intermitted to the last, to refer every specimen page and every title-page to him for approval, and no book could be carried forward or completed until the letters H. O. H. were upon these pages.

"The fact has often been commented on," says Mr. Houghton in his address on *Early*

Printing in America, " that the printing of
the first printers excelled in beauty of execution that of any subsequent issues of the
printing-press. The reason for this, I think,
will be apparent when we consider that the
first types were imitations of the chirography
of the monks, and from long experience and
practice this chirography had come to be very
beautiful; but, as was inevitable when speed
became an important element and the types
became mechanical appliances, this love of
beauty gave way, as has been the case always,
to utility and speed. The old German text,
also, through the process of years, has gradually given way to the more common Latin
text, and, as we see in the modern newspaper,
the process of deterioration still goes on in
obedience to the demands of haste. There
is a return now among the cultivated to the
more careful printing of earlier times. An
evidence that this early printing was, as near
as could be, transcripts of the careful penmanship of the old monks, can be seen in the
great folios in that remarkable library at
Cairo, where it is difficult even for an expert,

without close inspection, to say whether these books were printed or written."

A brief series of letters to his parents after leaving the University, and before setting up for himself as a printer in Cambridge, gives in a random fashion Mr. Houghton's apparently desultory occupation for these two or three years. The letters give also, especially to those who knew him in his later years, curious little intimations of his temperament, and of the resolute spirit which attended him in the early reaching out after a definite plan of life.

BOSTON, October 20, 1846.

DEAR PARENTS, — I found when I arrived in Worcester that the paper which had been sent me had been nearly a week on the road, and the situation had been filled up when I arrived, and therefore I came on to Boston the next morning. When I got here I found President Wheeler at the hotel where I stopped, and he gave me a very flattering recommendation, by the aid of which I have succeeded in getting a situation for a month at least in the *Daily Traveller* office, one of the best

papers in the city. My business is to be, if
I am prospered so as to do it readily, that of
reporter; that is, going about the city and
picking up the news and writing it out for
the paper, attending lectures and giving accounts of them. Perhaps I may come home
at the end of the month, and perhaps stay
longer. My salary is not very large at first,
but if I remain and succeed well it is to be
increased. I have found several acquaintances in the city, and by means of one of
them I obtained board in a private family the
first day I came here, so that it has not cost
me as much as it would at a public house; and
I have earned about two dollars in cash in a
printing-office, besides going on top of Bun-
ker Hill Monument, out to Cambridge, etc.;
and I am not at all sorry I came here; in
fact it seems to me providential.

I wish you would send me all the letters
and papers that have come for me since I left.
If you will pay the postage on the letters, and
get Mr. Russell or Johnson to do them all up
in one package, they will come cheaper than
they would separately, as they will then come

by weight. If you can send me some more stockings and my two best night-shirts by Mr. Russell, I should like it. They could probably find me at the *Daily Traveller* office on Court Street. I wish the letters directed "Traveller Printing - office, Boston." I am anxious to hear from you, how you are getting along, and I will endeavor to write again soon if you answer this immediately. I think I shall be able to send you papers occasionally. I am very much pleased with Boston, and have been treated very courteously and kindly by gentlemen who were entire strangers to me. I spent an hour or two in the library of the University in Cambridge, which consists of 52,000 volumes. I called on Mrs. Chamberlin yesterday, and found her quite smart.

Very affectionately your son,

H. O. Houghton.

Boston, October 13, 1847.

Dear Parents, — I am getting rather anxious to hear from you, as I have not heard a syllable since I left home. Neither have I heard anything from Marilla or Maria. Albert spent nearly two weeks in Boston, and has written to me two or three times since, short business letters. I bought a quantity of cranberries for him a few days since. He and his family sailed from New York about the first of October.

Soon after my return from home Mr. Dickinson sold a large part of his establishment, but I was retained in his employ and promoted to the office of proof-reader, which is about the highest notch as to dignity in the printing-office.

I saw in my paper last evening a little paragraph saying that a Mr. Haywood, a drover from Jaffrey, New Hampshire, had his pocketbook stolen from him, or else lost it, containing $3000 in bank-bills. He was in Brighton at the time. I feared from the description that it might be Elizabeth's husband. If so, they must feel very bad about it.

I wrote to Mr. Scott that you would send him what cheese you could spare. Mother, if you will knit for me, or get them knit for me, three or four pairs of good substantial socks,

I will pay you 50 cents a pair, or any price you please. I want them knit long, so that they will come up to the tops of my boots. I have a quantity of old clothes, such as my old overcoat, pantaloons, etc., which I would like to send home, if you would wish them, but I hardly know how to send them. I have not seen Russell this fall; has he been down yet? I hope he will call on me when he comes. I think my health is growing better, if anything. I am anxious to know how you are getting along, and I hope you will write to me, if not more than two lines, and direct Dickinson's Type Foundry, 4 Wilson Lane, Boston. My earnest prayer is that your last days may be made comfortable, and when you leave this world you may be prepared for a better habitation in another.

Affectionately your son,

Oscar.

Boston, September 2, 1848.

Dear Parents, — You will notice, by a circular that I sent to-day, that I have changed my place of business, as I intimated I might do when at home. Business declined at the Boston Type Foundry, so that they thought they could not afford to keep two proof-readers, and of course I was discharged. They expressed themselves perfectly satisfied with me, however, and gave me a letter of recommendation. Mr. Rand made me an offer soon after to come into his office and take in extra proof-reading, by which arrangement, if I am prospered, I hope to do better than I have been doing.

The *Traveller* folks told me they wished to send me to Worcester to attend a Democratic Convention next Wednesday. If there are any delegates from your quarter, please to send some word by them.

Did Daniel come home this summer? Why did he not come to Boston? Albert is not coming this summer, and Mr. Ready has not yet arrived. Do not fail to let me hear from you soon, and direct care of G. C. Rand & Co., No. 3 Cornhill.

Affectionately your son,

OSCAR.

P. S. I went on Wednesday last to Plymouth, and put my foot on the rock where the Pilgrims landed.

The following is the circular referred to in the previous letter : —

A CARD.

TO PRINTERS, PUBLISHERS, AND AUTHORS.

The undersigned, formerly proof-reader in Mr. S. N. Dickinson's stereotype foundry, has taken a desk in the office of G. C. Rand & Company for the purpose of accommodating those printers who may need extra assistance in proof-reading, or whose business will not warrant the constant employment of a professional reader. By this arrangement, it is believed, proofs can be read with promptness and dispatch, and at about the same expense as in the office where the work of composition is performed.

If a long and varied experience, the facilities afforded by a regular collegiate education, and a thoroughly practical knowledge of printing, may tend in any degree to inspire confidence, it is hoped the undertaking may meet with encouragement.

Attention given, also, to the preparation of manuscripts for the press when desired.

REFERENCES. — Mr. S. Phelps ; James M. Shute, agent of the Boston Type and Stereotype Foundry; C. C. P. Moody, former partner of Mr. Dickinson ; Messrs. Freeman & Bolles ; Messrs. Andrews & Punchard, editors of *The Daily Evening Traveller ;* and a large number of authors and publishers.

N. B. For reading first proofs, an intelligent boy provided to read copy without extra charge.

H. O. HOUGHTON.

No. 3 CORNHILL, BOSTON,
August 29, 1848.

BOSTON, November 16, 1848.

DEAR PARENTS, — I was very agreeably surprised one morning in finding a letter on my desk from mother. I know not who brought it there, but I have not had such a treat for some time past. I thank you for your invitation to Thanksgiving, and designed to avail myself of it; my business, however, is of such a nature that I cannot tell possibly whether I can be there or not on that day. But I hope to be permitted to drop in upon you in the course of two or three weeks. I went to Connecticut, and made James[1] a visit

---

[1] An older brother, Rev. James Clay Houghton, of Granby, Conn.

on Saturday last. I found them all well.
They have a fine girl, some ten months old,
with a white head and a deep-blue eye. James
was away on Sunday, and did not return until
Monday, and I had the visit with his family
all to myself. I returned to Boston on Tuesday, after having had a very pleasant time.

I have recently had an offer to go into business here which seems to me very favorable.
Mr. Freeman, of the firm of Freeman & Bolles,
who are among the best printers in the city,
if not the very best, has offered to sell me one
half of the office for $100 down and the rest
in yearly payments of $250 each. He esti-
mates that the half of the office will be worth
about $3000, which is to be left to referees
to say. Messrs. Little & Brown, who are the
most extensive publishers of law books in New
England, if not in the United States, propose
to make a contract with us to do all their
printing that we can do, at a stipulated price,
which will probably of itself be sufficient to
keep a large establishment in operation. They
are building a large office in Cambridge, the
rent of which is to be about half Freeman &

Bolles are now paying in the city. Mr. Bolles has been in business here about twenty years, and offers to put his experience on a par with my education, if I will go in with him. Gentlemen here in the city have agreed to sign a note for me, by which I can raise $500 or $600. Persons here who are acquainted with the business tell me that it is a good opportunity, and that we can probably make $2000 a year clear of expenses. Mr. Scott[1] and James both speak very favorably of it, and James tried to raise some additional funds for me, but did not succeed. I will try and come home soon, and tell you more about it. Till then adieu.

Affectionately your son,

H. O. Houghton.

P. S. Albert has a daughter a month or two old. They call it Maria, I believe. Mr. Scott's family are well. He said nothing about the cheese. I have not heard from Marilla for a long time. Write soon. I am almost out of socks.

[1] Mr. David Scott, his brother-in-law.

The last of these letters shows Mr. Houghton just on the eve of establishing himself in business with Mr. Bolles, but still lacking the funds needed to complete the bargain. There is a story that he was at work on the morning of the day when the option was to expire. There was a rap at the door, and, in response to his "Come in," there entered a countryman, who inquired, "Is this Oscar Houghton?" He was told that it was. "Well, now, Oscar, I'm right glad to see you," said the stranger; "my wife Sarah said that when I came to Boston I must be sure and see her cousin Oscar." The visitor proved to be a well-to-do New England farmer. He inquired after his relative's affairs, and Mr. Houghton told him of his plans, and stated that the hour had come when he must give an answer to the offer made him, but that he must give up the chance for lack of the needed money. "How much do you lack, Oscar?" asked the farmer. "About five hundred dollars," was the reply. Whereupon the visitor, who had become thoroughly interested, offered to make up the amount in a loan. As nearly as can now be known, the amount which Mr. Houghton raised was fifteen hundred dollars, one third of which was raised from friends on his promissory note, one third was lent by Mr. David Scott, and one third by his cousin's husband, Rufus Heywood, of East Jaffrey, New Hampshire.

The office was first established on Remington Street, in Cambridge, and a glimpse of the activity of the new business is seen in a paragraph of a letter to one of his sisters, written from Cambridge, March 5, 1849: "Your favor dated February 10 was not received until this evening. I had business in town, and went to the post-office and found it advertised. You know, I suppose, that I now live in Cambridge, and when you write again please direct there. I should be much gratified to see you, and hope I may have the opportunity before you leave on your mission. I have been designing to visit home, if permitted so to do, about the first of April, but it would be very difficult for me to leave now. We have about thirty persons in our employ, are chock-full of business, and hardly

ILIAD

settled yet. Please to let me know your plans definitely, as I am very desirous of seeing you before you go."

A year later he was writing to his parents:

CAMBRIDGE, February 18, 1850.

DEAR PARENTS, — I am getting quite anxious to hear from you, and I write with the hope that you will give me a few lines in return. Daniel was here a few days ago, and left here for Dana, and I suppose he told you all about me, and perhaps made a sorry story. I sent a gold dollar by him for mother, which I trust he delivered. Our business has given us a good deal of trouble, both before and since I was home, but we are getting along more smoothly, I think, now; and I am confident, with the help of Providence, we shall prosper. The "strike" will, I think, work to our advantage in the end, as we get better prices now, and are driving a heavier business than ever. I suppose you saw in the *Traveller* an account of the "striking" one of our women received some time since. There has been quite a noise made about it.

I received a letter from Maria a few days since ; she appeared to be in fine health and spirits. The Sioux had all gone a-hunting, and she and Mr. Hancock had gone 200 miles further north among the Winnebagoes, where the thermometer stood the first week or two in January at 27 and 30 degrees below zero.

, We shall look for Albert in March. I think I shall try and coax him to go home. Harriet appears to be getting along finely, and likes Boston and Boston people much better than she did. Her father wrote that she might come home with Albert in March, but she wrote back she did not wish to go until fall. Harriet Fyler is keeping house this winter for Governor Collier, and has not yet gone to Wetumpka.

Do let us hear how you are getting along, and if you are in need let me know it. May the Lord help you is the prayer of

Your affectionate son,
Oscar.

The religious expression at the close of this

letter was not a mere form of words. Mr. Houghton in his earliest years had been under the influence of the Congregational church, but the example of his eldest sister led him to cast in his lot with the Methodists. During his college days his reading and thinking had at one time led him to question the doctrinal basis of his religion, and he was inclined for a while to the Unitarian statement; but he worked out the problem with the result of becoming more securely established on the foundations of his early faith, at the same time that he acquired a habit of mind which gave him intellectual sympathy with a wide range of religious expression. Dean Huntington, of Boston University, wrote of him: "He did not care always to do what was simply conventional, or the thing that some one else expected him to do, but he had clear ideas of duty as he saw it, and this duty he was glad to do with all his strength. His type was ethical. The emotional kind of piety did not affect him deeply. He laid the emphasis of his belief upon integrity, justice, frugality, self-

respect, and charity to the suffering and
needy." It is a confirmation of the sturdy
character of his loyalty to the Methodist form
of religion, which he believed to be the most
practical order and the freest from the perils
which beset institutional religion, that he never
swerved from an identification with it, though
the engagement to be married, which he
formed at the beginning of his career, was
with a member of the Congregational Church;
and he was brought into intimate and very
admiring relations with her family, though
he married afterward a member of the Baptist
communion, and though, as years went on,
his wife and some of his own children passed
over into the Episcopal Church. The intimate
connection with the Methodist Church, though
it brought him into positions of service and
responsibility in the denomination, did not
restrict or narrow his sympathy. He had a
very great appreciation of the work of the
American Board of Commissioners for Foreign Missions; and he was wont to dilate
upon the admirable organization of the Rom-
ish Church, as well as upon the great impor-

tance of the contention of that church that
education of the young should be primarily
religious. It was not merely that his business brought him into close relations with
intellectual men of various creeds, and that
his business sagacity forbade him to make the
lines of his enterprise coincide with the lines
of his ecclesiastical relationship, but his nature
was catholic in its sympathy; he was at once
too large a man to be narrowly sectarian, or
to be religiously indifferent.

Upon first coming to Boston he had connected himself with the Bromfield Street
Methodist Episcopal Church, and after establishing himself in Cambridge, he returned for
a while to that church home. Dr. Warren,
now President of Boston University, was pastor of the church during a portion of that
time, and writes: —

" He was the Assistant Superintendent of
the Sunday-school of the Bromfield Street
Church when, with less than four years' experience in the ministry, I was sent thither to be
the pastor of such men as he, and of yet older
and riper saints, such as Mother Monroe,

Jacob Sleeper, Isaac Rich, David Snow, and others of their generation. Mr. Houghton was already a man of mark in the goodly congregation that filled the house. It was natural that it should be so. He was a man of liberal education, clear-headed, warm-hearted, prosperous in business, one of the comparatively few who came to church in his own family carriage, driving all the way from his Cambridge home, yet ready to remain to attend the Sunday-school and to do his part in the work of the church. Whenever I now think of those days, and realize that he was riper than his pastor by ten or more years of Christian experience and of world-experience, I marvel that he could have listened so attentively, and that he could have evinced his friendly feelings in such manifold and encouraging methods as he did."

There was another reason why Mr. Houghton clung to his Boston connection. He had made the acquaintance of Miss Elizabeth Harris, and the acquaintance had ripened into love, so that an engagement of marriage took place; but Miss Harris was frail in health and was attacked by consumption, a more distinctive New England disease then than now, and died, so that the marriage did not take place. Many of Mr. Houghton's friends will remémber the strong and kindly presence in his household of Miss Mary Harris, "Aunt Mary," as she was familiarly known, the real aunt of Miss Elizabeth Harris, and the titular aunt of the young family that afterward grew up under her eye, for she made her home with Mr. Houghton for many years before her death; the respect and affection he had for her, and the confidence she had in him, were manifest to all who knew the two together. How much this beautiful connection meant may be seen from the impulse which led Mrs. Houghton to give to her eldest daughter the name of Elizabeth Harris.

IV

THE quarters in Remington Street soon became insufficient for the growing business, and there was need of a more substantial establishment. As has been seen, the most important connection of the new firm was that with Messrs. Little, Brown & Company, of Boston, then as now an eminent publishing house, especially of law books. The moving spirit at that date was Mr. James Brown, a warm friend of the elder John Murray, from whom he named a son, who has succeeded him in business. Mr. Brown gave the young printer substantial encouragement, and by his advice and aid Mr. Houghton, who was now by himself, became Mr. Brown's tenant in a brick, domestic-looking building on the banks of the Charles River. The building had formerly been used by the city of Cambridge as a house for the town poor, and stood almost in the open country. Mr. Brown had bought the estate, and the building, after being re-modeled, was occupied by the firm of H. O. Houghton & Company. Mr. Houghton and Mr. Brown were desirous of giving the new press a significant name, and tried various experiments, till Mr. Brown said one day: "This press stands by the side of the Charles River; why not call it 'The Riverside Press'?" and this most natural name was then given it, so that now the term Riverside has come to cover a thickly populated district, and to be applied to various neighboring industries.

It was in 1852 that the firm of H. O. Houghton & Company was established at the Riverside Press,[1] and on September 12, 1854, Mr. Houghton was married to Miss Nanna W. Manning, who was at the time a teacher in the Cambridge High School. The first house occupied by the couple was in Ellery Street, but shortly after, by the aid and with the wise advice of Miss Mary Harris, he built

---

[1] An old payroll book shows for the first week, ending January 18, 1849, a list of sixteen names, aggregating $74. The increase of the business is seen by that for April 10, 1852, when there were fifty names and a total of $575.22.

the house on Main Street, now Massachusetts Avenue, still the home of the family. He added an apartment easy of access on the ground-floor for the use of his parents, who came to live with him. His mother died in 1858; and his father afterward went to the home of William Houghton, the oldest of the sons, in Nunda, where he died.

There was a period, therefore, of about ten years when Mr. Houghton may be said to have been establishing himself. He was married, had a house of his own, and saw a young family growing up about him. He was in full control of a printing-office; for though he did business under the firm name of H. O. Houghton & Company, the company was a friend who had embarked money in the enterprise and assumed no share in the management. He was in close relation with the Harvard Street Methodist Episcopal Church, where he was Superintendent of the Sunday-school,[1] and

---

[1] He was Superintendent from 1850 to the end of 1853. For several years after that he resumed his connection with the church in Boston, but returned to the Harvard Street church in 1862, was then made a trustee, and resumed his office of Superintendent in 1864, retaining it till his death. .

he was taking his part in the government of the young city of Cambridge as a member of the school committee, as well afterward as a member of the Common Council and of the Board of Aldermen.

There were two connections which he maintained in business that were of great importance to him. The firm of Little, Brown & Company, besides being very large law publishers, took the lead in enterprises calling for a good deal of capital. They planned and carried out a series of dignified historical and political works, of the kind to which we easily give the name of monumental, like the writings of John Adams and John Quincy Adams, and the speeches of Daniel Webster. They undertook also that long series of *British Poets* and *British Essayists*, neat, sober volumes in black cloth, each preceded by a steel-plate portrait of the author. A few of the volumes of the *British Poets*, those least in demand, like the poems of Bishop Heber, were simply small editions from English sheets bound uniform with the others; most of the books, however, were passed under the critical supervision of Professor Francis J. Child, with occasionally the aid of Mr. C. E. Norton and Mr. James Russell Lowell, and reset and stereotyped here. Much of this mechanical work fell to Mr. Houghton, and he was brought thus into friendly relations with the editors, and into very close relations with Mr. Brown, whom he always looked upon as the most far-sighted and courageous publisher whom he had known, — a man who saw his business in a large way, and yet had the resolution and decision to keep clear of speculative ventures. "Mr. Houghton," the elder man once said to him impressively, "never hesitate to stop any enterprise which is not paying : if you see a part of your business to be unprofitable, cut it off, no matter how much it hurts ; " and Mr. Houghton laid the advice to heart.

The other house with which the young printer made an alliance was the firm of Ticknor & Fields, which was rapidly acquiring a list of books in general literature, and making friends amongst English and American authors, especially of poetry and belles-lettres generally. If the volumes of the *British Poets* stood for substantial standard literature, the decorous brown-clad volumes with blind side-stamps will even now bring up delightful associations in the minds of readers who were young men and women in the decade of 1850–1860. When, a few years ago, the old firm name of Ticknor & Company was revived for a short time, Mr. Howells, with the enthusiasm of reminiscence, urged the new firm to hunt up the old-fashioned die, get some brown cloth made of the pattern of the old, and burst forth in a sort of resurrection suit, with the expectation of creating a genuine furore among book-lovers.

As Mr. Brown in the one house had been the one to take the initiative, so Mr. Fields, with his love of literature, gave direction to the list of the other; and, as good books demand good printing, he had very frequent recourse to Mr. Houghton. But the two men were nearer of an age than were Mr. Houghton and Mr. Brown, so that the relations were of a different sort; and Mr. Houghton was so confident of himself in his own art that he took the position of an adviser in mechanical matters, and not always that of a mere executive agent of the publisher. Once he invited Mr. Fields to look at a shelf of books in his counting-room. He had collected a number of the recent publications of Ticknor & Fields, and ranged them with special reference to showing the irrational irregularity of sizes of paper used in the manufacture.

For Mr. Houghton was devoting himself with the greatest ardor, not simply to the development of his business, but to the improvement of his art, and in doing this he was governed by a few broad, fundamental principles. I have spoken already of the clearness with which he saw the correct proportions of a page, and how pleased he was at finding that what his eye saw to be correct, a canon of architectural proportions confirmed. By a similar direct judgment, he early and always protested against the use of sizes of paper except the old, accepted dimensions, and regarded any departure from these as a futile attempt to secure individuality. He tried to enforce system and regularity in this respect into the books which he made for his customers; and when he had the power to order, as he did later in his own publishing house, the canon of regularity in paper was one which he would not have infringed.

He carried the underlying principle of beauty through simplicity into his typography. He at once discarded the customary typographic ornaments, though he pleased himself later when he was in England with having devices and initial letters designed expressly for him by a daughter of one of his printing friends, Mr. Whittingham. He discarded also the common expedients for securing variety by means of change in type; his aim was, not to startle, not to distract, but to make his type so clear, simple, and orderly that it should do its plain work of expressing language with the least ostentation. In all this he was helped by the constant handling of the best English books of the day, and he studied the work of Aldus, Bodoni, Baskerville, Pickering, and other master printers; but it is to be noted that he went straight to the mark from the start, and had apparently no false notions to get rid of.

It is not easy for the book-lover of to-day, accustomed to seeing well-printed books, to appreciate the important contribution which Mr. Houghton made to the art of book-making in America. There were other good printers contemporaneous with him, such men, for example, as Mr. Alvord and Mr. Trow, but no one seems to have emphasized with such distinction the few but fundamental laws of good printing, and he had, as we have shown, the occasion at his hand in his close association with two important publishers of the best literature. After all, the force which lay behind this manifestation of an art was the character of the man himself. He knew a good thing in printing, and he was not the man to give up his knowledge to the opinion of any one else. He was so much more positive than most of his customers, and he impressed his own convictions on them so determinedly, that he had his own way; his tenacity and his energy made him a most effective reformer in printing when he was engaged strictly in minding his own business.

His management of the printing-office was

marked by an unwearying attention to every
detail, and, hard as he made his men work, he
worked harder than any. On one occasion he
found himself drawn into contention with his
compositors. They made demands which he
thought were unreasonable, and they seemed
to have the advantage of him in the situation.
He quietly went about amongst some teach-
ers and other well-educated young women in
Cambridge, persuaded them to put themselves
under his tuition, privately trained them to
set type, and, when the battle seemed to have
gone against him, suddenly appeared with his
reinforcements, established them in his composing-room, and from that day to the end
not only had no further strike, but gave to
the entire composing-room a character for industry, skill, and courtesy. He was one of
the first to demonstrate on a considerable scale
the practicability of the employment of women
in this capacity; and it was characteristic of
him that he should draw to himself the best-
educated and best-mannered girls, and not be
aiming for the lowest-priced. He long had a
proof-reader, Miss Harris, on whose services
he set a very high value.

V

THE reputation which Mr. Houghton made, not only as a printer of singularly good taste, but as a prompt man of business, attracted to him other publishers than those already named, and made his office the favorite one of the small class of connoisseurs in printing who wished to secure a specially choice result in private publishing. One of the most interesting connections which Riverside made, and fruitful in the end, was with Mr. O. W. Wight, a scholarly gentleman, who was also a man of means, and adopted a mode of gratifying his tastes, and at the same time making his money earn interest, which I have often wondered is not more commonly followed. He was a lover of Montaigne, Pascal, Madame de Stael, and Voltaire, and he edited, I believe in part translated, writings of these authors, and resorted to Mr. Houghton as a printer who could make his books as beautiful in

page as he could desire.   Mr. Houghton made
the stereotype plates, as he might have made
them for any author, and then Mr. Wight
farmed them out to this or that publisher,
who bore the cost of printing, binding, and
selling, and paid Mr. Wight a royalty for the
use of the plates.   I do not attempt to name
all the books which Mr. Wight made in this
way, but his last, most considerable venture
was a new edition of Dickens, which long remained as the best example of Mr. Houghton's
art, and no one can now come upon an early
impression of the Household Edition of Dickens, as it was called, without being delighted
with the classic beauty of the page.   It was
for this edition that Mr. Darley made a series
of careful India-ink drawings, the originals of
which have long hung on the walls of Mr.
Houghton's house.

In all these projects Mr. Houghton took a
most active part, lending his judgment and
skill in planning the mechanical treatment,
and advising respecting the publication.   He
was studying all the while to enlarge the
circle of his connection with publishers, aware

of the risk he ran if he tied himself too closely to any one. Moreover, his independence and his consciousness of mastery in his own art made him impatient of any relation which left him only the position of agent, and he found himself often placed, as he thought, at a disadvantage. Not only did his transactions with Mr. Wight bring him into very close dealings with publishers, and familiarize him with the publishing side of book-making, but out of the difficulties which arose in these transactions there seemed but one way of wise escape, and that was into the assumption himself of the publisher's function. He needed an outlet for his manufacturing enterprise, and he felt increasingly the disadvantage of stopping short with the production of a book. The publication of the Dickens was in itself a serious affair in those days, for it was comprised in a long series of volumes.

It was under these circumstances, when his mind was gravitating toward publishing, that his business brought him into frequent intercourse with Mr. Melancthon M. Hurd, then a partner in the house of Sheldon & Com-

pany. The business of this house was mainly
in school books, and Mr. Hurd's taste and
interest were in the direction of literature.
The friendship of the two men, and their
common tastes in the matter of books, easily
led to the proposal of a partnership under
the firm name of Hurd & Houghton.[1] They
reasoned that New York was fast becoming
the great centre for the sale and distribution
of books, as of other merchandise, and that
not only was Riverside already well equipped
for the printing of books, but that Cambridge
must long be a natural meeting-ground for
authors and editors. There were long conferences in those days before and after the
inception of the new firm, and Mr. Houghton
was full of ardor in this enlargement of scope.
As, in the case of printing, he did not regard
his business merely as a support and means
of enrichment, so now his mind was given to
a forecast of the great field which lay before
him in the business of publishing. He meant
emphatically to make good books, to spare no
effort to make them pleasant to the eye and

[1] The "notice" of the partnership is dated March 1, 1864.

the touch, — that he was sure he could do, — and to be sure that they were wholesome and worth making beautiful. The new firm meant to cultivate new authors, but the list of books with which they began, books which for the most part had grown out of Mr. Houghton's connection with Mr. Wight, — Bacon, Cooper, Dickens, Montaigne, Macaulay, and others, — naturally opened the way for that attention to standard literature which always since has characterized the house. A year after the firm was established, it was announcing a portly library of old divines, to be edited by the former University of Vermont scholar, Professor W. G. T. Shedd, and five volumes of South's sermons was the result. Mr. Houghton also, from his great familiarity with the making of law books and his knowledge of the profitable nature of the business as then conducted, determined to make the publication of law books a specialty. He was more encouraged to this by the acquaintance he had formed with law writers, and by his intimate relations with Judge Bennett. He had, moreover, a natural proclivity toward the science of law. It appealed strongly to his robust, argumentative mind.

I do not know the exact order of events, but very close to this important step in Mr. Houghton's career was the business engagement he made with the house of Messrs. G. & C. Merriam of Springfield, the publishers of Webster's Dictionary, who were, I think, at this time ready to begin the production of a new edition of that work. Mr. Houghton knew very well that, however carefully he might keep the firm of H. O. Houghton & Company, printers, distinct from that of Hurd & Houghton, publishers, he was running the risk of losing engagements with other publishers by entering their domain himself; and he was too far-sighted to think that he could at once build up a publishing house which would exhaust the capacity of his printing establishment, so that he looked upon this alliance with G. & C. Merriam not only as good in itself, but as giving great stability to his manufacturing enterprise. He was aware of the fluctuations which attended the fortunes of miscellaneous publishing, and of the speculative element which inevitably attached to this business, and he valued highly this very important connection. The men on both sides were admirably joined. They were upright, honorable men, and they were also exceedingly able business men, unflagging in their attention to details, fair in dealing, but as keen in their bargains as they were faithful to their engagements. A life-long friendship grew up among them, which found many opportunities of expression outside of immediate business engagements. Several years later Mr. O. M. Baker became connected with the Springfield house, and much of the detail fell upon him. At the time of Mr. Houghton's death he wrote these words, which bear witness to the strong human relations which sometimes are formed within the shell of business : —

"During the whole eighteen years of my acquaintance with Mr. Houghton he has always impressed me as being my friend, even in the discussion of vexed questions where our interests were quite at variance, and I never had an interview with him that did not leave me with a feeling of the most profound respect for his manliness. It has been a source of much pleasure and satisfaction to me that I have seemed to merit his confidence and friendship; but I could be as nothing to him in comparison with what he has always been to me, and there is no one left, outside of the members of our firm, that I can go to with the same familiarity and confidence that I have so many times gone to him."

The formation of the new firm, and the demands created by the large contract with the Messrs. Merriam, called for an increase of facilities at Riverside, especially in the matter of a bindery, and in the spring of 1864 Mr. Houghton made his first journey to Europe. His errand chiefly was to secure master binders, and to open the way for securing the best material both in binding and in types. Necessarily he made himself acquainted at once with the wages paid to workmen in his own craft, and, since he was not only a practical printer but a man of education, he took a very strong interest in the economic and political questions which a comparison of the conditions in England and in the United States suggested to him. He had, as a Henry Clay Whig, accepted the doctrine of protection when he was a student in college, and had never seen any reason to change his mind. His experience in London did much to confirm him in this economic belief, and he used often to speak of the profound impression made upon him by the evidence which he saw of the almost hopeless prospect of the English workman as compared with that of his American fellow. A few years later, when the question of Protection *vs.* Free Trade was stoutly debated by Hon. W. D. Kelley, the veteran champion of protection in Congress, one of the workmen whom Mr. Houghton secured at this time wrote the following letter to Mr. Kelley: —

CAMBRIDGE, MASS., May 10, 1872.

HON. W. D. KELLEY, —

Dear Sir, — A fellow-workman having lent me a pamphlet containing a speech delivered by you, March 16, 1872, against free trade, I take the liberty of addressing you, as I am interested in that subject. Sir, let us

ILIAD

look at the blessings of free trade where it
works so well. I cannot do better than take
my own case. When in England I always
had a great desire to come to this country,
not that I expected to get rich, but wanted
to be able to save something for my mainte-
nance in my old age. In 1857 we began to
save. In 1864 Mr. H. O. Houghton was in
England, trying to engage some compositors,
printers, and book-binders. I am a book-
binder, and applied to him to see if he would
pay our passage, — myself, wife, and two
children. He came to Derby and I told
him what I could do. He agreed to advance
our passage money. We had been saving
nearly seven years; had twenty-four shillings
per week, which was the best wages given. I
had saved only £12 10s.

What is the difference between my life
there and that which I enjoy here? Mr.
Houghton lent me money to buy furniture,
and with the passage money I was in debt for
$270. I received $15 per week first; have
been advanced several times; now I have $22
per week. I paid the debt, have my life in-

sured and $615 in the bank. This has been done in less than eight years. You mention Hon. H. O. Houghton speaking of the compositors of England not being able to pay their passage; there were about twenty in the same shop with me, and not one married man better off than myself. . . .

Respectfully yours,

JAMES WILSON.

The new firm of Hurd & Houghton began at once to use the term "Riverside" in characterizing a series of books they projected, the Riverside Classics, and the custom grew of giving the title to editions in which special care had been taken to secure beauty and dignity of form, but always with a reserve in its use. Mr. Houghton, with the traditions of older printers before him, obtained from Miss Whittingham, in London, a monogram in which the two H's of the firm name were linked together, and used it on the title-pages of books. He had found a crest of the Houghton family, but he did not like the motto, which was somewhat truculent, and supplanted it with another, *Tout bien ou rien,* and used this phrase on his book plate, with satisfaction in its concise statement of his business creed; it was not till about 1880 that the motto began to be used deliberately by the publishing firm.

VI

My own acquaintance with Mr. Houghton
—though I had seen him once, a few years
before, when I consulted him about the
printing of a college magazine, of which I
was an editor — began in the year 1864,
upon occasion of the printing of a life of
an older brother, which I had written. It
chanced that the plates of the book were
made just before Mr. Houghton made his
connection with Mr. Hurd, and, as I intended
publishing the book at my own risk, I placed
it naturally with the new firm. I had previously appeared as the author of two books
for the young, and was intending to occupy
myself with literature. The acquaintance,
begun during the composition of the memoir
of my brother, which took me frequently to
Riverside, quickly ripened into friendship;
and when the new firm of Hurd & Houghton
was established I was asked to be the reader

of the manuscripts submitted for publication, and the critic of such English books as they might arrange to republish. As my home was in Boston, I was more frequently in Mr. Houghton's company than in Mr. Hurd's, though my reports were sent to the New York office. To be in with the formation of a new publishing house, when it already enjoyed the prestige of the foremost printing house in the country, as regards mechanical work, offered a pleasurable excitement to a young littérateur, and I took frequent occasion to walk out to Cambridge at the end of the day and visit the Press. Mr. Houghton then, as long afterward, found his greatest recreation in riding or driving, and it was not long before we fell into the habit of taking long drives together in the late afternoon, supplemented by a weekly dinner with the young family on Saturday. As my connection with the house became more intimate, the intercourse with the head of the house increased. Sometimes we rode together, sometimes we drove; and, as years went on, the son, who has now succeeded his father, was stowed away in a little seat in the buggy, until one day his father suddenly woke to the fact that the boy was growing up, and stopped our conversation to enjoin upon him the necessity of not repeating anything he heard us saying. The rides and drives after a while diminished, as Mr. Houghton's own family came to be his friendly companions and I had my separate family interests; but the peregrinatory conferences were resumed in recent years, when we were both living in Cambridge and having the same office hours in Boston. We looked forward to the spring, and to the fall after the summer diversions, when we could again walk out over the West Boston Bridge; and when the Harvard Bridge was built we found a new delight in the sunsets, which interrupted our talk as the western sky was brilliant above the noble sweep of the Charles River. Mr. Houghton, at the beginning of our connection, was fifteen years my senior, but the thirty years which slipped away found this breach closing, for we had established so many common causes that he came to ignore the difference

in age more even than I : that is one of the
privileges of the senior in such associations.

One of the first subjects which we discussed was the natural one of an organ of the
new publishing house. The fact that such
slight experience as I had enjoyed in literature was mainly in the direction of writing
for the young had something to do, no doubt,
with his resolution to undertake a magazine
for young people, but he was incited to it
also by the opportunity which it afforded the
Press. He was ambitious of doing superfine
work. It was an era when book illustration
was making very rapid advances. The University Press had achieved some notable suc-
cesses, and Ticknor & Fields, then the most
prominent publishing house in Boston, had
made a mark with *Our Young Folks*, an
illustrated magazine. Mr. Houghton thought
he saw in the publication of a similar magazine an opportunity to show what he could do
in good printing, and he was besides genuinely interested in the organization of sound
literature for the young. He saw how largely
English juvenile books filled the bookstores,

and he had a hearty and honest ambition to supersede them with books instinct with American life. He may have overstated the case, for he was impatient of nice distinctions when he had a point like this to make, but he was sincere in his adherence to protective principles, not only on the ground of self-interest, but on the more substantial moral ground of securing the greatest possible independence for America, and of fortifying the social institutions of the country. He used to repeat with great earnestness a criticism which Agassiz once made to him of a children's book in some department of natural history, in which every illustration was drawn from some object not native to America, and he denounced the ordinary English juvenile books as assuming the unalterable relation of classes as they exist in England. Such books, he declared, were unwholesome reading for American children; and he was for driving them out, partly by a tariff which discriminated against them, and partly by the production of native books which should supplant them as objects of merchandise.

A magazine seemed to offer the most familiar mode of exploiting juvenile literature, and so he planned a monthly which should be generous in proportions and wholesome in its character. There was much discussion over the name to be given it, and, after many proposals had been made and rejected, we fell back on the most obvious one of *The Riverside Magazine for Young People.* I say most obvious, and yet the term had not then been applied much further than to the Press itself, except in the case already mentioned of the Riverside Classics; but Mr. Houghton had at once a pride in the name, and a jealous regard for its fame. He had, when the magazine was started, a little shyness about its use; but he had already perceived its value as a trade-mark, and he found it a grateful substitute for the use of his own name, which he did not care to see used superfluously in the conduct of business. Indeed, the impersonal character of the word "Riverside" was its great value in his eyes. It stood for something objective, gathering his ideals, his aims, his honorable ambition, so that he could

enjoy and glory in it without any shame-
facedness. " Riverside," he once said to me,
" is like a diamond which I can hold up before my eye, and turn it this way and that,
and let the light fall on it, and see it sparkle."
In this saying he unconsciously disclosed the
secret of his power. He grew prosperous in
the conduct of his business, but the prosperity
fell to him because he was seeking something
higher. He was building an institution; he
was creating something which should have an
organic life of its own, and the whole stream
of his energy passed into this external creation. He projected himself into it, and never
withdrew his hand, but he thought of it as an
artist thinks of the picture he paints, the poet
of the poem he writes.

As I have intimated, the secret of Mr.
Houghton's power in business lay in the relation which he bore to his work: he was not
thinking of himself and his own aggrandize-
ment, — he was thinking of the institution he
was creating, and by a paradox, though he
threw himself heart and soul into the enterprise, he effaced himself to a remarkable

degree. It was impossible that so positive, so vigorous a personality should not be conspicuous in the business, and yet he shaped his industry with distinct reference to the growth of an organism. He was by nature and temperament a leader, and was impatient of anything like divided authority, but he was equally aware of the need of an order with clearly defined responsibility. In arranging his business, therefore, even when it was small and he carried all the details in his head, he insisted upon such a system of reports as should almost imitate the methods of an army. "If I tell a boy to hang up my overcoat, I expect him to come back and tell me he has done it," he would say, and his memory for details was extraordinary. An error, especially one arising from carelessness, committed by one of his young men, might have been forgotten in the course of time by the one who committed it, but Mr. Houghton never forgot it, and never allowed the young man to forget it. Abstractly considered, there was something comically terrible in this supervising memory, but in reality many a one, though withdrawing as far as he could into some recess of exculpatory consciousness when he saw the familiar reminiscence making for him, was rendered distinctly less capable of repeating his blunder, or making another like it.

As the range of the business increased, Mr. Houghton continued the system by which every operation came regularly under his eye. At first not a letter was written or a bill made out that did not pass before him for inspection before it was sent out, and when this minuteness of oversight became physically impossible, he continued to have a daily report of the correspondence made to him with a memorandum of the contents and the names of the persons to whom the several letters were assigned, and it was a familiar sight to see him going from desk to desk with a strip of yellow paper containing these memoranda, and acquainting himself with the condition of affairs. In the complexity of a great printing and publishing house there are multitudinous details, and the chance of error in some particular which shall confuse the result is very great. It was partly the necessity of meeting this condition, partly a native passion for thoroughness, which made Mr. Houghton extraordinarily alert and vigilant. "Follow it up" was his watchword, and his persistence in getting to the bottom of every difficulty, in fixing the responsibility of a mistake, was unflagging, his memory for derelictions most tenacious. The vigor of this discipline was very great and many chafed under it, but it was never relaxed, and no one was more completely subject to it than Mr. Houghton himself. It led him to the printing-office often early in the morning, before his men had arrived, and late in the evening again, to see that all was safe for the night. If he made rules, he was strenuous in enforcing them on himself, but he did not make many rules; he was not a martinet in discipline: he demanded obedience to the great laws of order, accuracy, thoroughness in all that was undertaken, and he aimed at simplicity rather than complexity of method.

Indeed, he was sometimes a little impatient of method, he believed so much more in the man behind the method. The most perfect method he knew would never execute itself; and when an elaborate plan was outlined, he spent little criticism on the plan, but wished to know at once who was to carry it out. Hence his attack, for failure in any enterprise, was directed upon the person who had failed, and few there were who escaped being hauled over the coals, as the expressive phrase is. The coals were rarely allowed to burn into dead ashes; they were fed by many occasions, and the hauling was performed with an energy which kept the hand well in practice. Mr. Houghton sometimes lost his temper in this exercise, but usually he drew back from the edge, and the person who was a disinterested bystander could often extract a vast deal of entertainment out of the racy speech which enlivened the reproof. Mr. Houghton's good sense of humor was his safeguard at such times, and his felicitous comparisons, his shrewd epithets, his remote anecdotes, all tempered the severity of his judgments. He showed, moreover, not infrequently, a singular faculty for conveying his meaning by the most casual and indirect speech, which was curiously incon-

sistent with the vigor of his direct attack. I
remember one of his associates coming out of
his room one day and saying : " Well, I have
been talking with Mr. Houghton for half an
hour, and I know just what he thinks, but
I 'll be blessed if he has said a word which
could be taken as an explicit expression of
his opinion."

It is a proper comment on this statement
of Mr. Houghton's manner toward his associates and employees that he kept by him year
after year the same persons. They were often
sorely vexed, — no chastisement for the present seemeth joyous, but rather grievous, —
yet it was rare that one of them deliberately
withdrew from his post. There were two or
three reasons for this : the person at fault felt
the justice of reproof; there was a positive
esprit de corps; discipline, however severe,
is apt to have something of a tonic virtue
in it; but above all, I think there was a genuine recognition of the inherent justice and
generosity of Mr. Houghton's nature, and an
assurance that there was nothing personal
in the retribution which he visited upon the

delinquent. Mr. Houghton used to say, earnestly, that he never discharged a clerk and never would. I used to think, sometimes, that there was not much to choose between an abrupt dismissal and a slow freezing out; but there was this marked difference, that the ordeal to which one was subjected might, and sometimes did, result in a distinct induration of the temper, so that a very effective workman was the result, and every one felt confidence that he would not be the victim of arbitrary action, or suffer permanently from an impulse of his employer.

It was a characteristic saying of Mr. Houghton that when the Press was crowded with work, he busied himself most with seeking new work. He was forearmed against the danger of over-confidence, and he knew that every harvest meant a time of sowing long before. But he was, above all, unceasingly mindful of the need of keeping the Press occupied. As a man of business, he knew the importance of making his machinery earn money uninterruptedly; as a captain of industry, he never forgot the company he had mustered; that work should be slack was a misfortune, but that thereby men should be thrown out of employment was a disaster, and he strained every nerve in dull times to find work with which to keep his men along, even though he had to take it at prices which yielded him little or no profit.

This solidarity of the Press, so that Mr. Houghton lived to see the grandchildren of some of his first workmen employed side by side with their grandparents, was further illustrated by one or two measures which he took for confirming the close relation he held with his workmen. He pondered long the expediency of making his growing business one of coöperation formally, and went so far at one time as to have papers drawn up for incorporation, providing for a pecuniary interest of all engaged in the business. But he was not a theorist: he was a business man with an idealistic tendency, and he had a stable mind which guarded him against a too experimental habit. Moreover, he could not help seeing that his own temperament would make it difficult for him to enter into engagements which might abridge his instinctive governing power; and finally, when the matter assumed a tentative shape, he did what a wise man will under such circumstances, — he heeded the voice of his wife, who threw the whole weight of her judgment in the opposite scale. But, though he did not change a partnership into a corporation, he could not rest content until he had devised some means by which he could bring every one in the Press into possible interest in the business, and the shape which his plan took was that of a savings department, by the terms of which any person employed could deposit savings and receive a good rate of interest, and, upon every even hundred dollars deposited, there might be at the end of the year a dividend if the business prospered, but a limit was set to the amount of this dividend. It was not coöperation in the technical sense of the term; it was not profit-sharing as a basis of business management; but it was an experiment in the direction of a closer interdependence of employer and employed, a rough-and-ready device for getting over some of the disadvantages of the wage-system without loosening the control of the business by those who organized it, and had to bear the responsibility of successful conduct and the risk of adversity.

One of the few men now employed at Riverside, of the group that came over in 1864, is Mr. James Wilson, of the bindery, whose letter to Mr. Kelley has already been printed. I have asked him to jot down some of his recollections and impressions, and he writes in part as follows : —

" One of the things I noticed about Mr. Houghton was his attention to business: he was at the place early in the morning very often before we were, and often after we left at night.   One Saturday night I was gilding some books that were wanted; it was eleven o'clock, and I was alone.   He came into the old back room and said: ' Well, Mr. Wilson, I am sorry to see you at work, as I do like a man to have his Saturday night to himself.' I was the more struck with it because he had been working in the counting-room himself alone, and only seemed to think of me.

" There was one trait in Mr. Houghton's

character which will always stand out in the
memory of his early employees ; that is the
way he had of going to the men while they
were at work, and saying a few encouraging
words to each one. This caused a mutual
feeling of goodwill to exist between the employer and employees, so that all felt a personal interest in the welfare of the place.
This acknowledgment of the employees was
not confined to the Riverside Press, but he
would always have a kind word wherever he
met you.

" There was another good trait about Mr.
Houghton : if any of the workpeople were
away sick, he would soon miss them, and he
would make it his business to inquire about
them, and frequently go to see them. By
such acts as these he wound himself into the
hearts of the workpeople in a way that few
men have the power of doing."

Mr. Wilson speaks also, in his notes, of a
scheme which Mr. Houghton had at one time
of building houses in the immediate vicinity
of the Press for the use of the workpeople.
He carried out his design to a slight extent

by taking occasion, when enlarging the building, to remove some wooden houses which stood in the way, making a court, to which he gave the name of Daye Court, from the first printer in Cambridge; but he never carried the design very far, partly, I think, because he required at that time all his capital for his business, partly because he had strong convictions of the unwisdom of segregating the people. He visited with interest such establishments as that of Mame at Tours, and spoke appreciatively of the villages which had grown up about great printing-offices; but he was emphatic in belief that in our American life every family should have its own voluntary place in the general community, and take part in church, school, and politics quite independently of industrial relations.

For one illustration of Mr. Houghton's interest in workingmen in connection with social order I am indebted to Hon. Carroll D. Wright. The time referred to was long subsequent to that of which I have been writing, but the incident has its value in this place. "About 1882," says Colonel Wright, "Mr. Houghton submitted to me a proposition which I have always felt more clearly disclosed the breadth of the man's mind than would his regular business operations. He informed me that he had for some years had in mind the advisability of publishing a periodical weekly for the benefit of wage-earners. He wished to have the periodical first-class in every respect, — as well gotten up, as thoroughly arranged, and as well printed, as the best illustrated papers. He wished it to be of the size of *Harper's Weekly*, and to contain interesting matter for the employees of New England especially, — all industrial facts, put in an attractive way; the treatment of current questions on a broad and non-partisan basis; the discussion of questions that would interest organized and unorganized labor; information as to inventions, — everything, in fact, that could interest and enlighten the men and women who are employed in great manufacturing works. He wished to have the journal illustrated in the best way. His idea was to furnish persons, at their address, by mail, copies of the publication, first asking the proprietors of works

to submit a reasonable list of persons to whom
it should be sent free for a while, or on subscription lists furnished by employers, who
would be asked in the first instance to pay
the subscription for the sake of distributing
healthy labor literature among their people.
Mr. Houghton confidently expected that the
quality of the publication would soon result in
actual cash subscriptions to a sufficient extent
to pay all expenses. He knew, of course, that
such an undertaking would involve a large
expenditure of money, and that it would be
some time — two or three years perhaps — before any return could be expected in the way
of income for expenses. It was not in his plan
to make any money out of the enterprise, but
simply to establish a high-toned journal working in industrial interests. To accomplish his
purpose he proposed to raise a guaranty of
$100,000, the parties subscribing to the fund
pledging themselves to pay in at times such
sums as might be necessary for the support
of the scheme, and until it was on a paying
basis, that is, paying expenses; and in this,
after his own pledge of $10,000, he secured

other pledges, so that the total amounted to
$30,000. But Mr. Houghton was too good a
business man to enter practically upon his
plan until the whole $100,000, which he
deemed to be necessary, should be pledged.
It was impossible to secure more than the
$30,000.

"Mr. Houghton very kindly proposed that
I take the editorial and business management
of the periodical, — a proposition which at
once enlisted not only my sympathy, but my
cordial coöperation. I should have been glad
to join in any such plan, for I believe that,
if it could have been carried out, very great
good could have been done to all involved,
both employer and employee.

"In considering the plan which I have outlined, I was, of course, thrown very much with
Mr. Houghton, and I was greatly gratified to
see how thoroughly interested he was in the
elevation of those who work for wages. He
had the right idea, that is, that the truest elevation can come only from a broad enlighten-
ment, — from instruction, from knowledge of
conditions; for it was in the plan to bring

out not only conditions as they exist, but in comparison with other times and countries, — everything, in fact, that would give the workingman a true picture of industrial conditions and the conditions of production. I believe now that, could a sufficient number of employers be induced to become interested in such a plan as that suggested by Mr. Houghton, more practical good could be done than in any other way. Of course, the publication of official documents furnishes a certain kind of information, but not in the way to attract men who are not students of economic conditions. A popular, high-toned, illustrated labor paper, with capital enough behind it to assure its success regardless of the subscription list, would be an undertaking of the greatest value and importance. Mr. Houghton was far ahead of his time."

Mr. Wright's letter illustrates the imaginative side of Mr. Houghton's nature. He liked to project a scheme of this kind, connected with his business, but reaching much beyond the scope of a merely commercial enterprise, and the process of persuading himself of its practicability was often accompanied by the exercise of his persuasive power on others. He was given to thinking aloud, as he would say, and his active mind grasped certain desirable results, and then busied itself in working out the means to reach the end. Thus at another time he imagined a great clearing-house for publishers which should be under their own management and bring certain important functions of distribution into the control of the houses engaged in it, thus minimizing the employment of jobbers. Again, he pondered long the intricate questions involved in trade discounts and net prices. He was not one to allow his theories too far to govern his business action ; he drew back often when the time came for putting his theories to an explicit test. But when he was committed to any plan, especially if it was one he had carefully worked out, he had a tremendous resolution in carrying it into execution, and in those cases he inspired others with great confidence in him. Much of his remarkable success was due to a faith in himself, which confirmed the faith of others.

VII

THIS is a sketch of Mr. Houghton, and not of the house of which he was so long the head; but in order to give the reader a convenient chronological survey of the development of the business, I will set down in a paragraph the successive changes in the style and personal constituency.

The firm of Hurd & Houghton existed under the same name until 1878, but from time to time changes occurred in its personnel. In 1866 Mr. Houghton's brother, Mr. Albert G. Houghton, who had formerly been a merchant in Alabama, was admitted, occupying himself mainly with the interests in New York. Not long after the establishment of the *Riverside Magazine*, Mr. George H. Mifflin, a recent graduate of Harvard College, came into the service of the house. In 1872 both he and I became members of the firm. I retired after three years, preferring to give my time more exclusively to literary pursuits, but have ever since been identified with the editorial department of the business. Mr. Mifflin is just completing a quarter century of membership, and is the head of the house. Failing health led to the retirement of Mr. Albert G. Houghton in 1878 from active engagement; and Mr. Hurd, who for a similar cause had previously withdrawn from close attention to details of business, also retired. At the same time the house formed a combination with James R. Osgood & Company, the successors to Ticknor & Fields and Fields, Osgood & Company. Mr. Osgood represented this house in the new firm, and the style became Houghton, Osgood & Company. This consolidation greatly increased the list of publications of the house through the accession of the names of the great leaders of American literature. The premises in Boston formerly occupied by James R. Osgood & Company became the headquarters of the publishing department, and the books now bore the imprint of Boston and New York instead of New York and Cambridge. The firm as thus

ILIAO

constituted continued for two years, when Mr. Osgood retired, and the style of the firm became, in 1880, Houghton, Mifflin & Company; and, shortly after, the publishing headquarters in Boston were removed to 4 Park Street, and in New York to 11 East Seventeenth Street.   Mr. Lawson Valentine became a partner, and continued thus till his death in 1889.   In 1884 Mr. James D. Hurd, a son of Mr. Houghton's former partner, was admitted to the firm, but he died in December, 1887. On the 1st of April, 1888, three new partners were admitted, — Mr. James Murray Kay, who was born in Glasgow, Scotland, but subsequently had large business interests in New Brunswick; Mr. Thurlow Weed Barnes; and Mr. Henry O. Houghton, Jr.   Since that date, Mr. Barnes has left the business, and Mr. Oscar R. Houghton and Mr. Albert F. Houghton, sons of the late Albert G. Houghton, have been admitted to the firm, and have their residence in New York.

In all these various changes Mr. Houghton was the controlling force.   After the business was concentrated in Cambridge and Boston,

he gave up with great reluctance the special
oversight of the Press and made his headquarters in Boston. For a long time, however, he made it his practice to visit the Press
daily, and it was there that his real affection
in his work lay. I was walking home with
him one day, the spring before his fatal illness, when he was contemplating his address
on *Early Printing in America,* and he fell
on some reminiscence of his own occupation.
He half whimsically and yet with real seri-
ousness was disposed to regret that he had
allowed himself to be drawn from the simplicity of a printer's business into the complexity
of publishing. He sketched his career as it
might have been, — the perfection of all the
processes of making books; the enlargement
of his premises to meet the demands of his
business, and yet the centralization of the
business and its restriction to one great function. It was in a way the passing mood of
a somewhat tired man; but I realized how
strong was his passion for his early vocation,
and also how his mind fastened on a large,
concrete expression of his ideals. He used

in the vigor of his days to speculate on an old age spent in the country with a toy printing-office to play with. He never relinquished a close scrutiny of the style of his books; he labored with type founders and paper makers to secure the results he wanted, and one of his most satisfactory achievements was a particular font of type, which goes in the Press by the matter of fact name of Number Thirteen, but is coming to be recognized as the "Houghton" type.[1]

Nevertheless, it is not likely that he would, if hard pressed, have refused to admit that, in giving his mind more exclusively to publishing, he was following a course clearly marked out for him in the expansion of his energies; and, as the publishing side of his business came to absorb more and more the product of the Press, he identified the two interests and treated them as a whole. It had always been a marked element in the success of the Press that books there were treated, not piecemeal, but with careful study of the interrelation of the several parts; and it was only a more

---

[1] This book is printed from Number Thirteen.

comprehensive application of the same principle when he perfected the organism of a
manufacturing publishing house.

He often expressed the opinion that the
function which discriminated the publisher
from the manufacturer and the seller of
books was that of making books known, and,
as he found it necessary to concentrate his
attention upon the general conduct of the
business, and to give over the details of manufacturing to others, he made much of what
may comprehensively be termed " advertising." The details of this he intrusted to
others, and indeed the system followed was
scarcely in any sense his scheme; but certain
general principles he insisted on with great
earnestness, and, in two or three instances,
worked out plans which illustrated his conception of the most effective advertising.
Newspaper advertising he termed dress pa-
rade, and he did not greatly rely on it, for
he thought the real work was done when
knowledge of a book was brought immediately to the attention of the person who
might naturally be interested in this particu-

lar book; and he was constantly pressing, therefore, the intelligent collection of lists of names of probable book-buyers, to be classified for use in the forwarding of special circulars and bulletins. He devised, also, the system by which an author should be advertised, especially when a new book was to appear, by means of a circular containing a woodcut portrait, and a well-arranged statement of the author's writings. Out of this grew the Portrait Catalogue, which received the flattery of imitation in different quarters. He believed, also, in phalanxes of books, and, recognizing the great accumulation of titles in the firm's catalogue, he planned a series of special catalogues by subjects, which developed finally into a carefully classified list of publications, perhaps the latest important piece of work organized by him in his business.

It is a further demonstration of this attitude toward his work, what may be called the egotistic as contrasted with the selfish, that he was singularly indifferent to the element of competition. He had of course, in his business enterprises, to measure strength with his neighbors, but he was not greatly influenced by what they did. For example, he did not study closely the work of rival presses, nor scrutinize the lists of other publishers, and, above all, he had a very lofty sense of comity between publishers. He never would solicit an author who had formed connections with another house. "If he chooses to approach us," he would say, " well and good. We are at liberty then to treat with him. But we will not stir a finger to get him away from the publisher who already issues his books." And he carried this scrupulosity to its utmost limits, though he was aware that efforts were constantly made to draw away from him the writers whose reputation he had stimulated. He carried his favorite advice to authors, to keep their books together, so far that more than once he discouraged a writer who was dissatisfied with existing arrangements from coming to him. He was wont to use a pretty strong term, " loyalty," of those who held by him in spite of temptations to go after other publishers; but he recognized quite as strongly the reciprocal

relations involved, and, once an author was
"on the list," he would strain a point before
he would suffer a new book from the same
hand to go elsewhere, even though it might
fall below the standard previously set. And
here I venture the assertion that in nothing
did Mr. Houghton show more sincerely the
friendly interest he took in the authors who
intrusted their books to him than in the patience and candor he showed while the books
were yet in manuscript. He knew well the
business principle involved in the requirement
that the manuscript should be ready for the
printer, and that it was no function of a publishing house to edit for authors the books
it issued ; but in many an instance, when the
manuscript offered was not thoroughly acceptable, he would deal with it as a possible book,
and, by advice, encouragement, and criticism,
get the work finally into proper shape. It
was this temper, over and beyond the commercial spirit, which made him a representa-
tive of the best class of publishers. He was
not in the technical sense a literary critic, and
he was perhaps disposed to underestimate the

art of literature, but he had a strong sense
of what was enduring, and a very direct way
of appraising books. Especially, whatever
appealed to the broad, common interest of
men, and was helpful in its character, commended itself to his judgment.

It was in keeping with the largeness of his
ideals in business and his far-sightedness that
he did not require the demonstration of immediate success. If an enterprise commended
itself to him as sound, he was willing to wait
for returns. There was, indeed, something
very attractive to him in projects which were
based on broad, fundamental principles, and
would take time for their execution, and these
projects were all the more acceptable if they
took the shape of modest beginnings. He
felt his way with experiments, but he was constantly seeing the probable development. He
had the courage which comes from a large
·business imagination. At the same time no
one could be more resolute in a demand for
the cold facts in the history of undertakings.
He perfected a system of records by which
he could ascertain the exact history of every

one of his ventures, and carried about in his pocket for frequent reference what he called his Bankrupt List — a merciless showing of the books that were not paying. Great was the satisfaction when one book or another would slowly emerge from the list and take its place among those which had paid for themselves.

Perhaps the most significant illustration of Mr. Houghton's treatment of his business as an institution is to be found in a step which he took not long after the formation of the firm of Houghton, Mifflin & Company. He established a weekly council, to which he gave the name, half in jest, half to conceal its importance, of "The Powwow." To it he invited his partners, and those persons who were heads of departments in the business, or charged with special functions. He made out a formal order of business and appointed a secretary, who kept the records, which were read at each session. At the meetings the various enterprises of the house were discussed, especially the new books which were recommended for publication, and action was

taken which was held to constitute the policy
of the house. Such councils are no doubt
common enough in large firms and corpora-
tions; but I think it is an unusual course for a
house to invite subordinates, who have no direct pecuniary interest in the concern, into an
equal share in deliberations and votes which
definitely affect the conduct of the business.
Naturally this recognition of the interest of
subordinates in the welfare of the house led
to a caution on their part in asserting themselves. There was a mutual concession without any loss of independence ; and, though
friction might now and then arise, the weekly
conference, year after year, of the same men,
engaged in the same general work, effected
just what Mr. Houghton designed, — a solidarity of mind. He saw that each member
of " The Powwow " was likely to look at
every project not only from his personal point
of view, but with the consideration suggested
by the function he performed in the business,
so that there would be diversity of judgment,
and every plan would be subjected to a variety
of tests. He saw also that the discussion

would inform all the members of what was
going on, and lead to greater union of action,
a matter of great importance when the tendency of each was to become engrossed in his
own part of the business. In the early years
of "The Powwow" he not infrequently expressed to me his doubt whether on the whole
it was worth while; he was more than once
piqued by our criticism of measures, or rendered impatient by the expenditure of time
over plans when he knew what was wanted
and only wished to get it done. But, as time
wore on, these expressions of doubt grew less
frequent, and he threw more weight into the
decisions of "The Powwow." As in other
cases, he struck out in a course, upon which he
had deliberated, with decision but with modera-
tion, feeling his way, and perhaps only partly
aware of how much the step meant. But it
is clear enough now that he builded well, and
that the power of organization which he showed
at the beginning of his career, when he was
captain and a large part of the crew, always
looked toward the creation of an institution
so perfected in its parts, and so self-perpetu-

ating, that his final withdrawal in the fullness of time should not appear to disturb a normal action. Mr. Houghton died on Sunday. The Tuesday following was a holiday in the city; on the Tuesday after that "The Powwow" met as usual, and proceeded at once with the business of the week.

VIII

IT was a cardinal principle with Mr. Houghton to put all his eggs in one basket, and carry the basket himself. He had a clause in his early partnership papers, prohibiting himself and his partners from engaging in any other business enterprise, and for his part he asked no other pleasure or interest than that which grew out of the varied and constantly changing forms of his occupation. He loved travel, indeed, and most of all to take his carriage and horses and drive with his family for days into the country, visiting the regions dear to him from early associations, and it was a privation to him when he was finally forced to give up his horseback-riding. He made occasional trips to Europe, and he crossed the country twice to California. Often he would come home from one of his pleasure trips with great glee at having picked up on the way a printing job.

Yet, with his large ways of looking at his business, it was quite impossible that he should not concern himself with public affairs when they bore very direct relation to the printing and publishing interest. He took a very vigorous hand in the discussions which went on whenever a tariff bill was before Congress, and in 1870 especially, in conjunction with Dr. Henry Charles Lea, was conspicuous in the struggle which went on over the proposed admission of books free. He maintained with great earnestness that such a policy would be fatal to the publishing interest. His influence in this direction was great. His frequent visits to Washington, and his warm friendship with Senator Morrill, brought him into the very heart of the fight. But perhaps his most notable service in public matters was in connection with the movement for international copyright.

This movement was pushed energetically by the authors of the country, but the most effective work was done when the publishers and manufacturers of books coöperated with the authors. Congress shared in the custom-

ary slighting regard bestowed by practical
people on the literary class, and was more
disposed to pay attention to the men who
represented large industrial interests. Of the
authors, Dr. Edward Eggleston was the most
influential advocate of the measure; and of
the members of Congress, the most steadfast
was Senator Chace of Rhode Island, who, however, was obliged by illness to retire from
active participation before the final action.
Mr. Houghton was early interested in the
movement and was unremitting in his earnest
attention to the interests of the bill. He visited Washington repeatedly, conferring with
senators and representatives, and taking counsel with his associates in the enterprise. No
one who has not been engaged personally in
an effort to press through Congress a measure which appeals chiefly to a sense of honor,
and yet involves all manner of private and
industrial interests, can appreciate the need
at such a time, not only of resolution and per-
sistency, but of patience, of tact, of individual
handling of men, of removal of prejudice and
even of counteracting the indiscreet zeal of

associates. Moreover, there was not always entire agreement among the advocates of the bill as to the policy to be pursued when amendments were offered, and the whole period, from the presentation of the bill to its final passage, was one of great anxiety and alternate disappointment and hope. It was a hand-to-hand conflict, most of the work being done in and about Congress in personal interviews.

Mr. W. W. Appleton, who was himself actively engaged in the contest, wrote to Houghton, Mifflin & Company for his firm after Mr. Houghton's death : " The writer has the most pleasant recollections of many interviews during the long and at times seemingly hopeless contest for international copyright, and found Mr. Houghton ready and eager to aid the good work in any way. His judgment, experience, and personal effort did much to bring about the success attained." " Mr. Houghton," says Dr. Edward Eggleston, "was one of the very foremost of all that engaged in that struggle, whether we consider his activity, or his prudence, or his influence. I differed from him strongly at the outset in regard to certain questions about the structure of the bill, but he was always frank, and an opponent knew where to find him." And Senator Chace, writing to Mr. Houghton in the spring of 1891, says : "—— gave me quite a full account of what transpired in New York and Washington just before the final vote, and, after hearing his account, I should feel very remiss did I not say to thee that it is clear to my mind that the country is most largely indebted to thee for thy prompt and vigorous action.

. . . " I am writing to thee in great freedom and in confidence, for thee is one of those whom I have found all the way through to ˙be, not only clear-headed, but faithful to all interests. Now that the victory is achieved, I feel like giving thee full credit for thy great service to the cause."

Mr. Houghton was, in truth, the main dependence of the advocates of the bill, as regards New England especially. His cordial relation with the printing craft was of great service. At first he was opposed to what is known as the manufacturing clause, or at least was not strongly in favor of it. He soon saw, however, that the clause would give to the bill the strong support of the printers, and, with his own sincere belief in the principle of protection, he came to recognize the desirability of the clause. Later, when he had the opportunity to observe the reception of the act in England, he wrote home : " I am inclined to think, in the light of subsequent events, that it was a wise thing to do; and I have not hesitated to say to those interested here that, if they undertake to get that part of the law repealed, it will jeopardize the bill." He was present at the Authors' Dinner in London, held after the passage of the act, and, after commenting on the speeches there made, he adds : " I think we have made a great step in advance, and American authors are to reap largely the benefit of it; and this is as it ought to be. The era of cheap books should come in now, and American readers as much as authors should reap the benefit."

He had a very just appreciation of Senator

Chace's labors in behalf of the act, and was indignant at the apparent lack of recognition of his services after the passage of the bill. "When I consider," he wrote, "how much he has done; that, having nothing, not even the remotest connection with the publishing business or authorship, he gave so much time and so much intelligent effort without any possible motive of personal advantage to himself or political advancement, the fact that he is so thoroughly ignored has been, I confess, a source of great annoyance to me." When, therefore, an address to Mr. Chace, signed by publishers and authors, was proposed, he took the most active interest in forwarding the plan, — giving, indeed, great personal attention to securing signatures on the eve of his journey to Europe. He wrote as follows to Dr. Eggleston, June 20, 1891 : —

DEAR DR. EGGLESTON, —We shall transmit to Mr. Harper in a day or two the paper which you indited, with a good number of signatures, and signatures of a character with which, I think, you will be pleased. We are only waiting now for Mr. Whittier's, which we hope to get by Monday; and we trust the paper will go over early in the week. I want to repeat what Mr. Harper has suggested, — that it is important that you should head the letter; and I have already taken the liberty to say to Senator Chace that you have written it, and that we are going to insist that you shall sign it first. Since the death of my wife I have taken scarcely any interest in anything, but there has been no duty so grateful to me as to help in securing these names. The cordiality which has been expressed and the interest which has been manifested have been extremely gratifying, and I trust it will be gratifying to Mr. Chace himself. I have felt ever since the passage of the act, and before, that Mr. Chace's interest and labor in this cause have been practically ignored. This will enable us to remove any such impression, I trust, from Mr. Chace's mind.

I have said that he had not long been a resident of Cambridge before he was asked to serve on the school committee, and afterward took his place in the common council and the board of aldermen. He had in these offices shown such qualities, and his expanding business had made him so much of a figure in the city, that he was elected to the office of mayor for the year 1872. He entered upon his duties with resolution, and with a determination to give the city a prudent and economical administration; but he also took a large view of municipal life. It was a source of sincere pride with him that, under the impetus which he gave, the beautiful Fresh Pond was made a fine water-park, and the survey which he gave of the city's needs in his inaugural address was both broad and sagacious.

Mr. Houghton was not reëlected to the office, although he was a candidate for a second term. His successful opponent was one of the city officers, whose discharge for insubordination he had forced. It would be idle to rehearse a quarrel which most people have forgotten; but it is not out of place to say that the very conscientiousness and energy which Mr. Houghton displayed stood in the

way of his popularity as a chief magistrate.
He abhorred slackness and indifference, and
anything approaching a shirk, and, with his
self-contained independence and sense of authority, he pushed through such obstacles as
met him by the exercise of an uncompromis-
ing will. Such men do not make themselves
favorites in government, but the bracing effect
of this strong leadership was not soon lost,
and the patient care with which the mayor
examined every least concern which came before him was gratefully recognized by those
who needed his strong aid.

Mr. Houghton did not confine himself to
official service in the city. He was on more
than one commission, indeed, and he interested himself repeatedly in movements which
looked to the betterment of Cambridge. His
business reputation brought him also into
positions of trust, both as an officer of a bank
and in the care of private estates. It also
made him of service to the religious denomination to which he belonged. President Warren, of Boston University, has spoken of the
long connection which Mr. Houghton had

with that institution, and with the Theological Seminary which antedated it. "It was in 1866," he says, "that our Theological Seminary was removed from New Hampshire to Boston. Mr. Houghton favored its establishment in Cambridge. I well remember his taking me in his carriage to inspect certain building lots and tracts of land then for sale in this city, on one or another of which he recommended our trustees to build. Some of these I often pass, and never, I think, without remembering our visit in 1866. Our trustees, however, found all these suggested lots too small for their generous plans, and hence purchased thirty odd acres in Brookline. Later their plans were further modified by the founding of Boston University, and the adoption of the Theological School as one of a group of metropolitan professional schools clustering about a vigorous academic department. Mr. Houghton was not displeased that his original suggestion had not been acted upon, and when, in 1872, the projected School of Law required for its safe launching a 'guaranty fund' of $5000, he was one of the five men who pledged and ultimately gave $1000 apiece for this purpose. He was one of the earliest Trustees of the University, and for quarter of a century was faithful in his attendance upon its almost monthly meetings. As Chairman of the Standing Committee on the School of Law, he rendered a highly valued service. His personal knowledge of the leading lawyers of Boston and vicinity was uncommonly extensive and accurate. His judgment, moreover, was so sound and unbiased that I never had occasion to regret an appointment to that Faculty when he had previously recommended it. His intimate relation to the Dean of the School, Judge Bennett, as an early and lifelong friend, was also in many ways beneficial. To find for a successor in the chairmanship of this committee a man of equal qualifications will be a problem of no small difficulty."

One further form of Mr. Houghton's public spirit may be mentioned in the active part which he took in the organization and practical working of the Indian Rights Association. His friendly relation with Senator Dawes made him especially ready to coöperate with him, and he looked forward in the latter part of his life with genuine pleasure to the yearly conferences at Lake Mohonk. But the most moving cause of his interest was the ardor of Mrs. Houghton.

IX

Mrs. Houghton answered well the fine old name of helpmeet; for not only did she enter heartily into her husband's life in all their common domestic interests, she fortified it by her own independent but not foreign enterprises. As she became more released from close supervision of her household in the maturing of her children, she entered with the enthusiasm and irrepressible cheerfulness of her nature into philanthropic and semi-public concerns. She was an ardent friend of the movement for bettering the condition of the Indian, and she was a very strenuous opponent of the suffrage for women. Mr. Houghton, as I have said, entered with her into the former work, and he was in sympathy with her principles of anti-woman-suffrage; but a large part of the pleasure he took was in the intimate companionship with one so unselfish, so

full of life and devotion, who filled to the full
his own conception of a generous activity.

When Mrs. Houghton died, on the 13th of
April, 1891, there were those who with affectionate chiding were wont to say that, if she
had spared herself more, she might not have
been so summarily and swiftly carried away
by the attack of pneumonia which seized her;
but Mr. Houghton, while conceding the pos-
sibility of this, took the nobler view. " She
went in all over," he said, " in the matters
she was interested in. She did not spare herself. Perhaps if she had taken care of herself
she would have lived longer, but her life was
full; she was happy in her many occupations.
It is better so." He was led to speak of the
mistaken kindness which succeeded in empty-
ing the old of occupation and responsibility,
and recounted the experience of his own father, who had wasted away, he believed, from
sheer inanity, because those about him were
affectionately anxious to shield him from care
and labor.

He had himself, before his wife's death,
begun to be shaken a little in his firm health;

but, though he professed a desire to get some
relief from a confinement to business, habit
was strong with him, and, despite the share
of work he surrendered to his associates, he
found it hard to relinquish his hold upon the
lever. But his wife's death made a profound
impression upon him. The loyalty he always
felt for his friends was a sacred feeling as
regarded his wife, and the nearly forty years'
companionship had made her indeed bone of
his bone and flesh of his flesh, so that, when
she passed out of his life, strong as he was,
he felt almost a bewilderment. The physical
weariness, of which he had been little aware
in the strength of his will, now became known
even to him. He set out with his daughters
on a nine months' journey abroad, and wrote
back from England that he had not been
aware how worn out he was until he got away
from home.

The party traveled leisurely, spending much
of their time on the yacht Victoria, which
took them not only into northern waters, so
that they visited Norway and Sweden and
Russia, but later brought them from the Medi-

terranean to the West Indies on their way
home. Part of the winter of 1892 was spent
in Egypt. Mr. Houghton by no means relinquished his concern for the business in his
absence. He kept up a busy correspondence
with the house, and gave a great deal of attention to projects which called for coöperation with foreign houses.

Upon his return to America in April, 1892,
Mr. Houghton resumed his customary place
in the business, and, though he succeeded
in absenting himself a little more than formerly in the summer time, there was no very
appreciable diminution of activity until the
winter of 1894–95. He spent his summer,
as for several years before, at Little Boar's
Head, New Hampshire, and made occasional
excursions to Vermont, especially when he
was constrained by the good-natured com-
pulsion of his friend, Mr. Norman Williams, of
Chicago, himself an ardent Vermonter and a
summer neighbor of Mr. Houghton. A Vermont Association had been organized in Boston in 1886, and Mr. Houghton was president

until 1894, when he insisted on retiring. The chief function of the president was to preside at the annual dinner of the Association, and Mr. Houghton carried his thoroughness into his social as into his business duties, and strongly attached to him those who had the execution of the plans of the Association. One of these, Captain S. E. Howard, secretary of the Association, wrote to Mr. Houghton to congratulate him on reaching his seventieth birthday, and received this reply : —

BOSTON, May 18, 1893.

DEAR CAPTAIN HOWARD, — I have sometimes thought that if I were a military man and your superior officer, with power of life and death in my hands, I should order you to be shot. I feel a good deal like the boy I used to know in Vermont, who said he could bear anything except being "twitted of facts;" and to find one's self being congratulated upon being threescore and ten leads a man to be a little rebellious. However, I will forgive you for reminding me of it, and also will commute the old grudge which I had against you for allowing me to be continued as President of the Vermont Association. There is one advantage of being an "old fellow," and that is that one's friends can say how much they think of him while he is alive and kicking. One of the pleasantest things connected with my membership in the Vermont Association has been the pleasant friends I have made, and among them all there are none that I esteem more highly than you and our mutual friend, Colonel Carpenter, my co-workers. Wishing that you may live to be fourscore and ten or more, I am

Yours very truly,
H. O. HOUGHTON.

A complimentary dinner was given Mr. Houghton by the Association after he retired from the presidency, but at his request there were no reporters present, and what was said on that occasion was not preserved.

This recurrence to early memories was accompanied by a lively interest in family history, and in one or two letters written to a

friend at this time, Mr. Houghton gives a
glimpse of the manner in which he was using
some of his enforced leisure. He was particularly interested in the alliance which he was
shown to have with early printers.

CAMBRIDGE, December 28, 1893.

. . . I am much pleased that you are interested in my genealogical researches. Many
years ago, before my marriage, I fell in with a
man who had been to England to make special
researches about the Houghton family; and
from him I obtained the family tree, the coat-
of-arms, seal, etc., and, in looking over some
old papers recently, I discovered a copy of a
letter from John Burke, the author of Burke's
Peerage, addressed to Sir Henry Bold Houghton, an English baronet, informing him that
his family were descended from the Planta-
genet kings. The motto, I am sorry to say,
was a fighting one, " Malgrè le Tort," and
I changed it many years ago, retaining the
crest. At this Christmas, Miss Leach, of Philadelphia, — who with her father has been
helping me to formulate my ancestors, so that

I could join the Sons of the Revolution, as
well as the Society of the Old Colony Wars,
— has sent to me our family coat-of-arms,
which she has carefully and I believe accu-
rately marked out and painted and had
framed. For the Old Colony Wars I have
six or eight ancestors from whom I can
claim the right. And for the Sons of the
Revolution my son has one claim more than
I, as his great-grandfather on his mother's
side was chaplain in the Revolution.

January 11, 1894.

. . . Some years ago I was asked to speak
about printing at a dinner of the Harvard
Club in New York, and then and since I took
a great deal of pains to investigate the subject.
The principal authority is Thomas's *History of
Printing*, but the information was meagre and
confused ; but I got no hint from any source
of my relationship to the president [*i. e.* President Dunster of Harvard]. This was discovered by my friend, Mr. Leach, of Philadelphia,
who has made genealogy a study for many
years. The result of my investigations was,

that President Dunster was the first printer,
and not Stephen Daye. A clergyman by the
name of Glover, for the purpose of converting
the Indians, set sail from England in 1678
with his family, Stephen Daye (supposed to
have been a blacksmith), and the printing ma-
terials. Mr. Glover died on the passage. The
press was set up in President Dunster's house.
He subsequently married the widow of Mr.
Glover, and years afterwards his children sued
Mr. Dunster for an accounting, and Major
Willard was called in to settle the matter between the children and the president. Stephen Daye was discharged about the time of
Mrs. Glover's marriage, and a Samuel Green,
a native of the town, took the place of Daye,
and kept it for fifty years, while Daye turned
land speculator. Meantime President Dunster had a law passed by the colonial legisla-
ture that all printing required in the colonies
should be done in Cambridge. He also had
a censorship of the press appointed, and he
was one of the censors. Besides, when a com-
peting press was sent over, Dunster bought
it. So I infer that he was the real printer,

and rather an enterprising man besides.   Now
Major Willard, having lost his English wife,
married Elizabeth Dunster, a sister of President Dunster, and she dying he married Mary
Dunster, supposed to have been a younger sister or niece.   Mary Willard, a descendant of
this marriage, married Ensign Jacob Houghton, my great-grandfather.   From this union
of Willards and Dunsters came two presidents
of Harvard College, and some other fairly
respectable descendants. . . .

Although Mr. Houghton kept his place at
the head of the house and rarely missed a day
at Park Street, it was clear that he was con-
sciously relaxing the tension of his hold on
business details.   There was the same quick-
ness of perception when projects were discussed, the same faculty for going straight
to the centre, but there was less disposition to
watch closely the separate movements of the
great organism he had so long been building up.   With this relaxation there seemed
almost a release of that part of his nature
which in the strenuous activity of his life had

been held in restraint. With the sunshine of prosperity came a mellowness in which the warmth of his disposition showed itself in generous converse with his friends. As he sat in his office, he welcomed those who came on business as friendly visitors. It had been one of his marked characteristics that he never hurried a caller, and would sit leisurely chatting with him when his clerks outside were fuming over the interruption of what they thought important business; now he let his sociability have free play, and especially delighted when some old associate, under no greater pressure, as Dr. Holmes for example, who was a frequent visitor, could draw his chair beside him for a familiar chat. Always peculiarly open to the frank friendship of the young, as he grew older he turned instinctively to them for companionship. His daughters' friends found in his mingled courtesy and playfulness a charm which won their confidence and respect. A touch of his manner may be seen in a letter which he wrote to a neighbor shortly before his return from his last journey to Europe : —

TO E. W. C.

CAIRO, EGYPT, May 11, 1892.

MY DEAR EDITH, — Your kind note and the calendar enclosed were duly received at Christmas, and very gratefully so. The little sweet face on the Christmas card looked as if it was all ready to be kissed, as you were in days long agone. I do not know how to sufficiently compensate you for your charming remembrance unless I send you a camel. Would you like a young one or an old one? They both look very picturesque. I saw Alberta mount one for the first time on Saturday. He groaned and made a great fuss, but after a big effort he raised himself on his forelegs, and she swayed back and forth in true Oriental style. After she had succeeded, Elizabeth and Justine mounted their respective camels, and I a donkey! Their camels got up easier, but I had hard work to mount the donkey; the stirrups were too short and the saddle too high. You will see us all doubtless, in time, reproduced in photograph on our various mounts.

Please thank Miss B—— for her kind re-membrance also. I do not quite know what to bring her in return. I had thought of the Sphinx, but that would not do, as she is a woman and would not be appreciated; besides, she has got a battered nose, which indicates she may have been on a drunken spree in her early life. How would a young buffalo do? They are frisky and seem sociable, and have a way of depressing their horns on their necks so that they look very docile. . . .

We have taken passage to-morrow on Rameses the Great for the first cataract on the Nile. After that we expect to set our faces homeward. We trust a good Providence will give us favoring winds and speed us on our way, so that we may soon be able to greet all our dear friends. Please give my kindest regards to Miss B—— and C——, if he is not so inveterate a mugwump as not to care for them, and with love for yourself from your still

Young friend,
H. O. Houghton.

To the large circle of his nieces and nephews and their children, Mr. Houghton was increasingly bound by the interchange of friendly intercourse and by the frequent acts of kindness which he was able to show, and it is not strange that he was peculiarly drawn to his one living grandchild. He welcomed her advent with a quiet, happy pleasure which was good to see, and it was one of his great resources, as his life contracted in other ways, to visit her and watch her life expanding. When he was absent from her, he wanted news of her, and something of his eagerness to share life with her may be seen in this letter, written when she was an infant only, and he was back in the neighborhood of his own childhood : —

MONTPELIER, VT., December 24, 1894.

MY DEAR GRANDDAUGHTER ROSAMOND, — I received your sweet letter to-day, the first I ever received from a granddaughter, and I suppose the first you ever wrote. I must say that the penmanship, as well as the expression of your ideas, did you great credit. If you keep on improving until you are thirty you are likely to be the most famous female member of the Houghton family. Perhaps you may be allowed to vote on account of your great learning. To prevent you from being a "blue stocking," I think I was none too early in suggesting that we would have "high jinks" together as soon as you get big enough. I think this is important, as I do not want you to be too literary, nor do I think your grandmother, if she were living, would like to have you vote, but would much prefer you should be a sweet, healthy, rollicking little girl than a prudish, pale pedant, so please kick and jump just as hard as you can, so you can be in good training for us to have a lot of frolics together. Perhaps you will come up to Vermont with me some time, where there is in winter usually plenty of ice and snow. There is but little snow here to-day, but Aunt Alberta and Cousin James have just gone out to ride in a wagon, although the thermometer this morning was about down to zero. I was sorry not to see you before we came away, because you were asleep, but when you get older we will try and regulate these matters to suit ourselves. With love to your mamma and papa, and with ever so much to your dear self, I am

Your affectionate

GRANDPA.

P. S. Your photograph in your papa's arms is right before me, in which you appear to excellent advantage.

In the autumn of 1894 Mr. Houghton was affected by a difficulty of breathing, which greatly impeded the freedom of his movements, and kept him from time to time housed at home; so that, when the winter came, it was thought wise for him to go South, in hopes that a less stringent climate would give him relief. His eldest daughter went with him, and his family physician, also, as far as Asheville. He was restless and moved farther South, trying one place after another, only to return in the spring with the kind of new hope and courage which come to one who has done with travels for health, and is once more in his own home. A letter written when

he was making his way northward gives a
hint of his winter : —

TO CAPTAIN S. E. HOWARD.

LAKEWOOD, NEW JERSEY, April 2, 1895.

MY DEAR CAPTAIN HOWARD, — There is
something very good about you; whether it
is innate, or comes from your association with
Vermonters, I cannot say. It seems to be there
just the same, as evidenced by your thinking
of a poor fellow suffering from the grippe and
wandering about seeking for sleep and rest.
We first went to Asheville, North Carolina,
where for a few days everything seemed to
go well, when there came a succession of
rainy and cold days, when breathing was difficult, and sleep seemed impossible except by
stealth.   The local doctor told me I must
get out, and, as it seemed against his interest to have me do so, I did it.   He sent me
to Columbia, South Carolina, where I did improve in the sleeping and the weather was
milder, but the " fodder " was dreadful, — the
old Virginia style.   I stood it as long as I could,
and then we struck out for this place.   Here

Henry Oscar Houghton

we have comfortable quarters, high prices, palatable food, and a tendency to sleep added. I purpose to try this awhile, unless something drives me away from here. At any rate, I trust to be home about the middle of April.

Not long after Mr. Houghton returned to Cambridge, in the spring of 1895, there was a festival held by the Riverside Press, on the occasion of Mr. Mifflin's fiftieth birthday. The celebration was happily conceived and carried out by a committee chosen by the large body of some six hundred men and women who now made up the establishment. Mr. Mifflin himself knew only so much of the affair beforehand as it was necessary to confide to him. Mr. Houghton was apprised of the event and took a deep interest in it, but necessarily could have nothing to do with the management. When the day came, his family, ever watchful of him in his declining strength, debated whether he would be able to attend the festival, which was to be held in the evening. He listened without much comment, but in the course of the discussion he

quietly slipped out and went down to the
Press, where he held a consultation with some
of the committee; he had resolved that the
affair should be more significant than appeared
on its face.

It was agreed in his home that he might
safely venture to the hall for a part of the
exercises, and his carriage could wait to bring
him away if at any time his strength or his
interest flagged. Several times during the
earlier part of the evening, when speeches and
song and other entertainment were going on,
one of his daughters whispered to him a suggestion that he might easily escape, but he
smiled and thought he would stay through.
In fact, he had his own plans, which he had
no intention of subjecting to debate. A sup-
per was to follow, in the lower hall, and Mr.
Houghton quietly took his place at the head
of the procession. His daughters, surprised
at his endurance of an excitement to which
he had not seemed equal for several months,
were now overtaken with dismay and appre-
hension when he was called upon for a speech.
They did not know then that he had specially

asked the committee to call upon him; they feared only that his weakness would distress him and the audience if he attempted, with his wavering voice and struggling breath, to make even the simplest remarks.

Mr. Houghton rose to his feet with all the strength of his prime, and in a voice which was never firmer or clearer, with a manner direct and coherent, he told at length the story of Mr. Mifflin's association with him from the beginning, — giving him the hearty praise of one who had long tried him and had come, strong man as he was, even to lean on him. Many of the younger workers at the Press had never before seen Mr. Houghton; none of them ever saw him in his capacity of leader again. It was an open, frank, and loyal transfer of his mantle to the younger shoulders, — a plea that his successor might have the respect and support and fidelity of the men which had heretofore been given to himself. It was a fitting climax to a great career.

When the summer of 1895 came, Mr.

Houghton was advised not to expose himself
to the climate of the seacoast, and he availed
himself of the courtesy of Mr. Mifflin, who
placed at his partner's disposal his country-
seat at North Andover. There, in a quiet
rural district, Mr. Houghton could have not
only the seclusion of his own home, but the
pleasure of exploring the beautiful country
about the place. He took daily drives when
he was at home, but, with the unconquerable
energy of his nature, he persisted in frequent
journeys to the office in Boston. There was
something very pathetic, something also very
noble, in the resolution with which he clung
to his work. He had never known when
he was beaten; he did not know it now, but
kept up the attack week after week. His
daughters shielded him in every possible way;
his friends visited him; and the humor which
had so often turned the warm side of life
toward him did not fail him now.

There was, now and then, an acute form
taken by his disease which alarmed not only
those about him, but Mr. Houghton himself;
and, though he was not much given to pre-

sages, it was clear that he saw his end draw-
ing near. Without referring to this directly,
he made it somewhat evident by the seri-
ousness with which he collected himself in
occasional talks over important concerns. I
remember one such, which made a strong
impression upon me. It was the last day of
July, when he arranged to have me see him
by himself. There was a matter in which we
were both greatly concerned that had come
to the point of decision. He began, in his
characteristic manner, at a long distance from
the matter in hand. His words came with
difficulty, his attitude showed discomfort. He
rehearsed many situations and relations with
which we were both familiar, and came nearer
and nearer to the heart of the subject. His
manner deepened in earnestness, his voice became stronger, and he spoke with emphasis,
— with eloquence, indeed. In this matter he
could make no personal inquisition, as he had
been wont to do; he must leave it to the
decision of his partners. Yet the principles
which underlay the whole were insisted upon,
and he felt deeply the interest involved. He

was not thinking of his personal estate: he was
thinking of the institution he had founded;
that republic must suffer no hurt.

His strength failed him steadily, but he
made an almost superhuman effort on Fri-
day, the 23d of August, to be present at the
celebration of his grandchild's first birthday
anniversary in Winchester. It was as if he
gathered his strength for this final demonstration of his love and his indomitable will.
He returned the same day to North Andover,
and on Sunday, the 25th, he died.

After his death there were public expressions of appreciation of his worth and his
services. Resolutions of respect were passed
by the book trade, the bank in which he was
director, the University which he had so long
served, humane societies to which he had belonged, and the city of Cambridge. A memorial service was held at the Harvard Street
Methodist Episcopal Church, at which the
Riverside Press was represented by one of its
oldest members. Yet, when even a strong
man has died, one turns presently from these

public expressions, sincere as they are, for there begin to come to light the secret ways of the man's goodness. It was in the nature of Mr. Houghton's care for others that it was confidential. But a man's testament cannot be kept private, and it was quickly known that Mr. Houghton had established a generous fund to be administered by his daughters for the worthy poor of Cambridge. This act was not the tardy charity of him who can no longer use his wealth. He had been doing this kind of good for years, sometimes in direct relations, sometimes through almoners. He aided students struggling for an education; he gave liberally to his poorer kin; and there were certain discreet persons who received from him regularly sums of money for distribution. He was especially glad to do this through his church. "I cannot better put you in possession of what I have learned of his genuinely benevolent heart," said his pastor, Rev. George Skene, at the memorial service, "than by reading you a letter which I received from him a short time before he left us. He had from time to time placed in my

hands sums of money to be used in charity
as I found occasion. Appreciating the fact
that he was a business man, and systematic in
his methods of doing business, I was careful
to keep an accurate account of all disburse-
ments, and report to him in detail the disposition of his gifts. After my last report I
received this letter from him : —

"My dear Pastor, — I have your account of your stewardship, and find it very
satisfactory. I enclose herewith another
check, if it will not trouble you too much,
to use in the same way. When this is used
up, will you kindly let me know and call for
more? Thanking you for your kind interest
in distributing my little benefaction,
    "I am sincerely yours,
        "H. O. Houghton."

The last connection which Mr. Houghton
had with the office where he had so long
transacted the business of his life was to make
inquiry into the well-being of one of his ben-
eficiaries.